Textbook written according to revised syllabus of S.Y.B.Com.
prescribed by University of Pune from 2014-2015
Also useful for other universities in Maharashtra.

I0641205

Business Economics

Prof. Dr. Asha Khilare

Prof. Dr. Suresh Waghmare

Diamond Publications

Business Economics
Prof. Dr. Asha Khilare
Prof. Dr. Suresh Waghmare

First Edition : June 2014

ISBN : 978-81-8483-578-6

© Diamond Publications

Type Setting :
Diamond Publications

Cover Page :
Sham Bhalekar

Published by :
Diamond Publications
264/3 Shaniwar Peth, 302 Anugrah Apartment
Near Omkareshwar Temple, Pune - 411 030
☎ 020-24452387, 24466642

info@diamondbookspune.com
www.diamondbookspune.com

Sale Distributor :
Diamond Book Depot
661 Narayan Peth
Appa Balwant Chowk
Pune 411 030
Tel. - 24480677, 66020282

PREFACE

      It is a great pleasure for us to present this book on Business Economics (Macro) for the students of S.Y.B.Com of University of Pune.

      This book comprehensively covers the entire syllabus of Second Year B.Com. course of University of Pune effective from academic year 2014-15. The contents of the book are presented in simple and understandable manner. Also this book is a comprehensive and full-fledged text for S.Y.B.Com. Course. Maximum care has been taken to cover entire syllabus.

      We are very grateful to Mr. Dattatraya G. Pashte, publisher of Diamond Publications for giving us the opportunity and his co-operation in bringing out this book. We are also thankful to staff who have assisted and helped us in preparing this book.

      I earnestly hope that this book would fulfill the expectations of the readers. The suggestions of readers will be warmly welcomed.

With Best Wishes,

Prof. Dr. Asha Khilare
Prof. Dr. Suresh Waghmare

CONTENTS

PREFACE

<u>Term - I</u>

<u>Term - II</u>

Chapter 1	BASIC CONCEPTS OF MACRO ECONOMICS

CONTENTS

INTRODUCTION

The term 'macro' was first used in economics by Ragner Frisch in 1933. This term is concerned with the economy as a whole. Malthus, Sismondi and Karl Marx in the 19th century dealt with macro economic problems. Walras, Wicksell and Fisher were the modern contributors to the development of macro economic analysis before Keynes. Economists like Cassel, Alfred Marshall, Pigou, Robertson, Hayek and Hawtrey developed a theory of money and general prices in the decade following the First World War. But credit goes to Sir John Meynard Keynes who finally developed macro economics after the Great Depression.

1.1 MEANING OF MACRO ECONOMICS

The word 'macro' means large. Macro economics means economics in the large. Macro economics is the study of aggregates and averages covering the economy as a whole such as total income, total employment, national income, aggregate demand, aggregate supply, general price level and so on. In other words, it is aggregative economics. Macro economics studies the interrelations among the various aggregates, their determination and causes of fluctuations in them.

According to Prof. Ackley, "Macro economics deals with economic affairs in the large. It concerns with the overall dimensions of economic life. Thus, it deals with the major economic issues, problems and policies."

Prof. Boulding states that, "Macroeconomics deals not with individual quantities as such but with aggregates of these quantities; not with individual incomes but with the national incomes; not with individual prices but with the price level; not with individual outputs but with the national output."

Dornbusch and Fischer argued that, "Macroeconomics is concerned with the behaviour of the economy as a whole with booms and recessions, the economy's total output of goods and services and the growth of the output, the rates of inflation and unemployment, the balance of payments and exchange rates."

Samuelson and Nordhaus defined macroeconomics as "… the study of the behaviour of the economy as a whole. It exmines the forces that affect many firms, consumers and workers at the same time."

Prof. Culbertson argued that, macro economic theory is "… the theory of income, employment, prices and money."

Prof. Hansen defined macroeconomics as, "…. that branch of economics which considers the relationship between large aggregates such as the volume of employment, the total amount of saving and investment, the national income etc."

Thus, macro economics is that branch of economics which studies economic activities at the level of an economy as a whole.

1.2   NATURE AND SCOPE OF MACRO ECONOMICS

Nature of Macro Economics

Macro economics does not deal with the individual units like a firm but it deals with aggregates like national income, total employment, aggregate demand etc. It studies the problems related to the economy as a whole.

The objective of macro economics is to study the problems, policies and principles relating to full employment of resources and growth of resources. The goals of macro economics are a high level of output, low level of unemployment and price stability.

Macro economic analysis deals with the equilibrium between the forces of demand and supply of the economy as a whole. Aggregate supply and aggregate demand are expressed in terms of money as total income and total expenditure. Thus, aggregate demand and supply are related to total income.

Macro economics is first and foremost a policy science. Macro economics is basically a policy oriented subject. It deals with the macro economic policies to solve the problems such as poverty, unemployment, etc. faced by the economy as a whole.

Macro economics focuses on the economic behaviour and policies that affect consumption and investment, the rupee and the trade balance, the determinants of changes in wages and prices, monetary and fiscal policies, the money stock, the union budget, interest rates and the public debt. In brief, macro economics deals with the major economic issues and problems of the day.

Scope of Macro Economics

Scope of macro economics means the areas of study or subject matter of macro economics. Macro economics mainly deals with the following areas of study:

1) **Theory of National Income**: Macro economics studies the concept of national income, its different elements and the methods of measurement.

2) **Theory of Employment**: Macro economics studies problems relating to employment and unemployment. It studies different factors determining the level of employment.

3) **Theory of Money**: Changes in demand and supply of money have an impact on the level of prices. Macro economics therefore studies the functions of money and the theories relating to it.

4) **Theory of General Price Level:** Determination of general price level is one of the study areas of macro economics. Problems relating to inflation and deflation are important related areas.

5) **Theory of Economic Growth:** Poblems relating to economic growth is another study area of macro economics. Monetary and fiscal policies are also the subject matter of macro economics.

6) **Theory of International Trade:** Macro economics studies the issues related to international trade. Export, import, exchange rate and balance of payments are the sub areas underin.

7) **Theory of Business Cycles:** The capitalist economies suffer from business cycles. During the period of prosperity output and employment tend to remain at high levels, whereas during the recession periods both, the output and employment decline significantly which results into widespread unemployment.

1.3 SIGNIFICANCE OF MACRO ECONOMICS

Macro economics as a method of analysis has both theoretical and practical importance, as discussed below :

1) To Understand the Working of the Economy

Macro economic analysis helps in understanding functioning of the economy. Most of the economic problems are related to economic aggregates, such as total income total output, total demand, general price level etc. As these variables are measurable, their effects on the functioning of the economy can be analysed and necessary measures can be taken in time to avoid evil consequences.

2) Policy Orientation

Macro economics is basically policy oriented subject. It suggests most suitable policy measures, such as fiscal policy, monetary policy, income policy etc. to deal with complex economic problems, like unemployment, inflation, poverty etc.

3) National Income

Macro economics is useful for estimating and using national income data for the purpose of forecasting economic activities. It also helps in explaining distribution of income among different sections of the society.

4) Economic Growth

Macro economics provides basis for evaluation of growth performance of the economy. Plans are prepared to achieve increase in national income, output and employment for promoting economic development of the economy as a whole.

5) Business Cycles

Macro economics helps in analysing causes and understanding the effects of business cycles which take place in free enterprise capitalist economies. It also provides remedies to achieve economic stability in the economy.

6) Monetary Problems

Macro economics is useful for analysing monetary problems like inflation or deflation which adversely affect the economy. It suggests suitable policy measures like monetary and fiscal policies to overcome them.

7) Dynamic Science

Macro economics adopts dynamic approach to analyse economic problems and suggest suitable solutions also.

8) Macroeconomic Paradoxes

Macro economic paradoxes, such as paradox of thrift. Saving on individual level is a virtue but on society level it is a vice and the futility of wage cut policy as a remedy during the period of depression explains the importance of study of macro economics.

9) Issues of Vital Importance

Macro economics deals with the issues of vital importance, such as unemployment, inflation, instability of foreign exchange rates etc. which directly affect the well being of the people.

10) Decision Making

Macro economics helps in understanding the working of the economy as a whole, hence individuals and businessmen are able to take right decisions at a right time.

Limitations of Macro Economics

Macro economics has certain limitations. These arise mostly from attempts to generalise on the basis of individual studies. The limitations are as follows :

1) Fallacy of composition

In macro economics aggregate economic behaviour is assumed to be the total of individual activities. But what is true at an individual level may not be true on an aggregate level. For example, saving is private virtue but a public vice. If an individual depositor withdraws all his money from the bank, there is no problem, but if all the depositors withdraw their deposits at the same time, the banking system will collapse.

2) To Regard the Aggregates as Homogenous

In macro economic analysis, macro economic variables are considered as aggregates of homogenous components and individual differences are not taken into consideration. For example, inflation is measured as a change in the general price level, with the help of wholesale price index number. The changes in relative prices of different goods are not considered and only average price is taken for measuring the change in the price level.

3) Aggregate variables may not be important

It may be observed that the aggregate variables forming the economic system sometimes, may not be significant. For example, increase in national income may be the result of increase in incomes of rich people only. Such increase of national income may not be useful for estimating the welfare of the society as a whole.

4) Indiscriminate use of macro economics tend to be misleading

An indiscriminate use of macro economics for analysing economic problems may be misleading. For example, the policy measures adopted to achieve full employment, may not be suitable for solving the problem of structural unemployment in individual firms and industries. Similarly, measures adopted for controlling general price level may not be effective for controlling prices of individual commodities.

5) Statistical and conceptual difficulties

If individual units are homogenous aggregation becomes easy, but if the micro economic variables relate to dissimilar units, then their aggregation into one macro economic variable tends to be wrong and dangerous too.

In spite of these limitations, macro economics is useful for the analysis of economic problems faced by the economy as a whole.

1.4 DIFFERENCE BETWEEN MICRO AND MACRO ECONOMICS

The difference between micro and macro economics is as follows:

1) Basis of Study

Micro economics studies problems of scarcity and choice at the level of an individual, a household, a firm or an industry.

Macro economics studies problems of scarcity and choice at the level of an economy, as a whole. For example, micro economics studies problems such as consumer's or producer's behaviour and equilibrium while macro economics studies problems such as unemployment in the economy, problem of price rise, etc.

2) Degree of Aggregation

In micro economics, there is a limited degree of aggregation of economic variables compared to macro economics. For example, micro economics studies the equilibrium of an industry; it is an aggregation of all the firms producing a similar commodity whereas macro economics studies equilibrium of the economy as a whole; it considers aggregation of all producing units in the economy.

3) Different set of Assumptions

What is assumed as constant in micro economics is not constant in macro economics and vice versa. For example, in micro economics total output and employment are taken as constant. In macro economics distribution of income is taken as constant.

4) Central Issues

Allocation of resources is the central issue in the micro economics. On the other hand, level of output and employment is the central issue in the macro economics.

5) Method of Study

Method of study in micro economics is often described as 'partial equilibrium analysis' while method of study in macro economics is often described as 'general equilibrium analysis'.

6) Micro - Macro Paradox

What is true at the micro level may not be true at the macro level. For example, if an individual saves more, he faces future confidently but, if all the people in an economy try to save more demand for goods and services will decline. As a result, investment may decline; production and employment level may also fall.

The difference of micro and macro economics may seem well on the surface, but these two categories of study can overlap in significant ways. In fact, no one can understand economics well without micro and macro economics.

QUESTIONS

1. Define Macro Economics.
2. Explain the nature and scope of Macro Economics.
3. What is the significance of Macro Economics?
4. Discuss the limitations of Macro Economics.
5. What is the difference between Micro and Macro Economics?

Chapter 2

NATIONAL INCOME

CONTENTS

INTRODUCTION

National income is very important to a country because it shows how strong or weak the economy is. National income throws the light on distribution of income in an economy. It measures the level of economic activity in a year. The present unit focuses on the important aspects of national income like meaning and importance of national income, different concepts of national income, measurement methods of national income and difficulties in the measurement of national income, etc.

2.1 MEANING OF NATIONAL INCOME

The economists define national income in different ways. In simple words national income is the total value of country's final output of all goods and services produced in one year. In other words, national income of a country can be defined as the total market value of all final goods and services produced in the economy in a year. It means that national income is a monetary measure where physical quantities are converted into money terms. National income includes the market value of all final goods and ignores intermediate goods.

The concept of national income has three ways of interpretation. 1. It represents a total value of production, 2. It shows a total receipts and 3. It represents total expenditure. There is identity in all these three ways of interpretation of national income.

The amount received as national income is identical to the amount spent as national expenditure which is also identical to what is produced as national output. Therefore, the terms of income, output and expenditure are interchangeable.

From the above analysis it follows that:
National Income = National Product = National Expenditure

Importance of National Income

The study of national income is very important for number of reasons. Some of the reasons we explain for instance. National income data are of great importance for the economy of a country. National income data is the basis of national economic policies. The national income data is also useful for the economic planning. The researchers use this data very often to make their research useful. National income statistics helps us to know the per capita income as well as distribution of income in the economy.

2.2 CONCEPTS OF NATIONAL INCOME

There are various concepts relating to national income which we have explained below:

Gross Domestic Product (GDP) is the market value of the final goods and services produced within the domestic territory of a country during one year inclusive of depreciation. There are both resident as well as foreign producers within the domestic territory of a country.

Nominal National Income and Real National Income

Nominal National Income (National Income at current prices)

National income at current prices is the market value of final goods and services in the economy during an accounting year. Current year prices are the prices prevailing during the year of estimation.

National income at constant prices (National Income at constant prices)

It is the market value of the final goods and services produced in the economy during an accounting year, using the base year prices. Base year is the year of comparison when production and general price level believed to be normal. Money illusion can be eliminated with the use of this method.

1) Gross National Product (GNP)

Gross National Product is defined as the total market value of all final goods and services produced in a year in a country.

It is necessary to note that GNP includes only currently produced goods and services in a year means it is a flow measure.

GNP is one measure of the economic condition of a country. A higher GNP leads to a higher quality of living of a people in a country and vice versa.

2) Net National Product (NNP)

NNP is the market value of a nation's goods and services minus depreciation. Depreciation is often referred to as capital consumption.

The formula for NNP:

NNP = Market value of Finished Goods + Market value of Finished Services - Depreciation.

Depreciation means wear and tear of machinery in the process of production. Machines used for production have to be replaced in future course of time. Machines become useless due to their constant use over a period of time. Fixed assets are not permanent and therefore must be replaced to continue production process.

3) National Income at Market Prices and Factor Costs

National income at market prices means the money value of goods and services produced in a year which includes taxes and subsidies.

National income at factor cost is calculated by subtracting net indirect taxes i.e. total indirect tax - subsidy from NNP at market prices.

4) Per Capita Income

The per capita income is arrived by dividing the national income by population. Per capita income is measured either at constant prices or on current prices.

5) Personal Income

Personal income is that income which is actually obtained by the nationals of a country.

Formula of Personal Income:

Personal Income = National income - Undistributed Profits of Corporation - Payments for Social Security Provisions - Corporate Taxes + Government Transfer Payments + Business Transfer Payments + Net Interest paid by Government.

Transfer payments include pensions, unemployment relief, interest payment on public debt, etc.

6) Disposable Income

The personal income is the income of an individual. A person has to pay personal taxes, property taxes, etc. and after that whatever left to him is known as disposable income.

Formula of Disposable Income:
Disposable Income = Personal Income - Direct Taxes

2.3 MEASUREMENT OF NATIONAL INCOME

Circular Flow of Income

Circular flow of income involves different sectors of the economy. The economy is broadly classified into four sectors:

i) The Producing Sector
ii) The Household Sector
iii) The Government Sector
iv) The Rest of the World Sector.

These sectors contribute to the circular flow by performing different economic activities in the economy.

Let us see, how activities of different sectors play their role in the circular flow. In this context, we shall consider the two sector model of circular flow of income. In addition to this, there are other two models of circular flow 1) Three Sector Model and 2) Four Sector Model.

The circular flow of Income in a two sector economy

We consider a very simple model consisting of only two sectors. 1) the producing sector and 2) the household sector. We assume that there is no government sector as well as no foreign trade in the economy. It means that there is a closed economy. In this simple economy, the circular flow model will be as follows :

Model Circular Flow

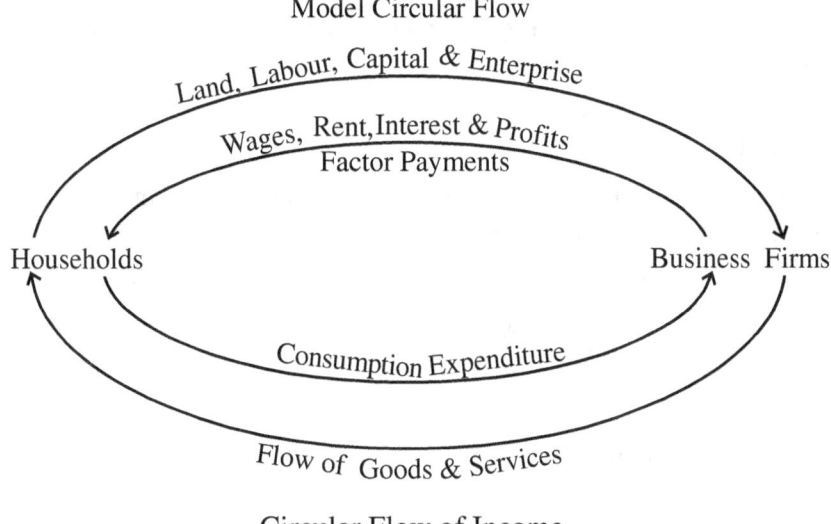

Circular Flow of Income

In the upper loop of the figure, resources such as land, labour, capital and enterprise flow from households to business sector as indicated by the arrow mark. In opposite direction to this money flows from business sector to households sector as factor payments such as wages rent interest and profits.

In the lower part of the figure, money flows from households sector to business firms sector as consumption expenditure made by the households on the goods and services produced by the firms, while the flow of goods and services flows in the opposite direction from business firms to households sector. Thus, it is clear that money flows from business firms to household as factor payments and then, it flows from households to firms as consumption expenditure. Thus, there is a circular flow of money or income. This circular flow of income will continue indefinitely. This is how the economy works.

One thing is important to note that the flow of income will not always remain same in volume. During the boom, the circular flow will expand and in depression this will contract. This is so because the flow of money is a measure of national income hence, it changes with change in the national income.

Assumptions of the Circular Flow of Income - two sector Model.

i) Economy consists of only two sectors - the business/firms sector and the households sector.
ii) Households spend their entire income means no savings.
iii) Closed economy means there are no exports and imports.
iv) No government sector in the economy.

We can draw the following observations from this model of circular flow:

a) Total production of goods and services by the firms are equal to the total consumption of goods and services by the households sector.
b) Factor payments by the firms are equal to the factor incomes of the households sector.
c) Consumption expenditure of the households sector is equal to the incomes of the households sector.
d) Money flows to opposite to the real flow of income. Factor services flow from households sector to the business firms sector is a real flow. Factor payments flow from business sector to the households sector is a money flow.

Real flow refers to the flow of goods and services across the different sectors of the economy. Money flow refers to the flow of money across the different sectors of the economy.

Thus, we have explained the flow of income that occurs in the functioning of the closed economy.

We have the three methods of measurement of national income.

1. Production Method
2. Income Method
3. Expenditure Method

1. Production Method

In this method, net value of final goods and services produced in a country during a year is obtained. This represents the gross domestic product. Net income earned in foreign boundaries by nationals is added and depreciation is subtracted from the gross domestic product.

This method of calculating national income can be used where a data of production is available for the year. This method shows the relative importance of different sectors of the economy by showing their contribution to the national income.

Production method is also known as output method or value added method. The total output of the economy is the sum of the outputs of every industry. However, since an output of one industry may be used by another industry and become part of the output of that industry. To avoid counting the item twice we use not the value of output by each industry but the value added i.e. the difference between the value of what it puts out and what it takes in. The total value produced by the economy is the sum of the value added by every industry.

The following precautions should be taken while using the value added method:

i) Value of the sale and purchase of second hand goods is not included because value of second hand goods is already accounted during the year they were produced.

ii) Commission earned on account of sale and purchase of second hand goods is included in this method.

iii) Own account production of goods is taken into account in this method because these goods are like those produced for the market.

iv) Value of intermediate goods is not included because it is already included in the value of final goods.

v) Value of production for self consumption is taken into account because these goods are like those goods which are produced for the market.

vi) Rent on the owner occupied house is also taken into account because all house have rental value.

vii) Service for self consumption in not included because it is difficult to estimate market value.

2. Income Method

Under this method the national income is obtained by summing up of the incomes of all individuals of a country.

Individuals earn incomes by contributing their own services and services of their property like land and capital to the national production. Therefore, national income is calculated by adding up wages, rent, interest and profits and income of self employed people. This method is useful to know the distribution of national income among various sections of the society such as land lords, capital owners, workers and entrepreneurs.

According to this method, national income is measured in terms of factors payments such as wages, rent, interest and profit to the owners of factors of production like land, labour, capital and enterprise during an accounting year.

Income method is also called the Factor Payment Method. A factor income refers to the income earned by a person as a reward for rendering his factor service in the process of production. A factor income may be in the form of wages, rent, interest and profit.

Sum total of factor incomes generated within the domestic territory of a country is called the net domestic product at factor cost.

The following precautions should be taken while using the income method.

i) Transfer earning like old age pensions, unemployment relief, scholarships should not be included because there is no value addition in the economy, but retirement pensions are to be included because these are the part of compensation of employees.

ii) Income from illegal activities like smuggling, theft, gambling etc. should not be included in the national income.

iii) Commission paid on sale and purchase of second hand goods to be included as this is the reward for rendering factor services.

iv) Brokerage on sale or purchase of shares or bonds is to be included in the national income.

v) Income from windfall gains like lottery should not be included as there is no value addition.

vi) Rent of owner occupied houses is to be treated as rent as a component of factor incomes.

vii) Production for self consumptions should be taken into account in this system.

viii) Corporate tax, dividends and undistributed profits are components of corporate profits hence any of these components should not be added separately.

ix) Income tax should not be added separately because it is paid out of compensation of employees.

x) Wages and salaries in cash and kind as well as social security contributions by the employers on behalf of employees are component of compensation of employees. Therefore, any of these should not be separately added.

3. Expenditure Method

Expenditure method is also called the consumption method. Expenditure method arrives at national income by adding up all expenditures made on goods and services during a year. We add up following types of expenditure:

1) Expenditure on consumer goods and services by households and individuals. It is denoted by 'C'. This is called final private consumption expenditure.

2) Governments expenditure on goods and services to fulfill the collective wants. This is called government's final consumption expenditure. It is denoted by 'G.'

3) Expenditure by enterprises on capital goods. This is called gross domestic capital formation. It is denoted by 'I'.

4) Expenditure made by foreigners on goods and services of a country exported to other countries called as exports and denoted by 'X'.

5) We deduct from exports (X) the expenditure by people, enterprises and governments of a country on imports (M) of goods and services from other countries. This is the net exports (X - M)

Thus, we add up the above four types of expenditures to get final expenditure on gross domestic product at market prices (GDP_{mp}). Symbolically, we can mention this as $GDP_{mp} = C + I + G + (X - M)$

Where,

C = Household consumption expenditures
I = Gross private domestic investment
G = Government consumption
X = Gross exports of goods and services
M = Gross imports of goods and services

Precautions for the Expenditure Method

The following precautions should be taken while using the expenditure method.

i) Only Final expenditure is to be taken into account to avoid error of double counting. Final expenditure means expenditure on final goods and services.

ii) Expenditure on second hand good is not to be included because value of second hand goods has already been accounted during the year of their production.

iii) Expenditure on shares and bonds is not to be included in the total expenditure as these are only paper transactions.

iv) Expenditure on transfer payments by the government is not to be included because such payment does not cause any value addition.

v) Estimated value of expenditure on goods produced for self-consumption should be taken into account. Also estimated rent on owner occupied houses should be taken into account.

The expenditure method focuses on the total output of a nation by finding the total amount of money spent. This is acceptable because like income the total value of all goods is equal to the total amount of money spent on goods.

All three methods of measurement of national income should in theory give the same final figure. However, in practice minor differences arise from the three methods for several reasons. One problem for instance is that goods in inventory have been produced therefore included in product method, but not yet sold therefore not included in expenditure method. Similarly, timing issues can also cause slight differences between the value of goods produced and the payments to the factors that produced the goods mainly if inputs are purchased on credit and also because wages are collected often after a period of production.

In the end we can say that though we can use any of the method out of three methods there is equality of figures of national income.

2.4   DIFFICULTIES IN MEASUREMENT OF NATIONAL INCOME

The correct estimation of national income is not an easy task. Difficulties of various kinds are faced in the measurement of national income. These difficulties are classified into two groups.

I) Conceptual Difficulties or Theoretical Difficulties.
II) Practical Difficulties

The theoretical difficulties appear in almost all countries. The practical difficulties are generally faced by the under developed countries.

Conceptual Difficulties

These difficulties relate to the various concepts of national income. Source of conceptual difficulties are as follows:

1) Determination of Intermediate and Final Goods : The national income of a country consists of only final goods and services. Final goods refer to those goods which are ready for the consumption. It is always not possible to make a difference between final good and intermediate good. For example, cotton used by a doctor is a final product but if it is used for making a shirt then it is an intermediate good.

2) Services without Remuneration: In our daily life we see a mother taking care of

her child, a housewife looking after a house and so on. No payment is made for such services. Therefore, they do not form a part of national income, but the same services are provided by a baby care taker and a house maid, payment will be made. So same services will be included in the national income.

3) Transfer Payments: Transfer payments refer to those payments for which a receiver has not to perform any economic activity. A pension paid by the government to the retired employee is an example of transfer payment. Such payments do not form the part of national income.

4) Pricing of Products : Valuation of the final product is a difficult task. We know prices change every month, every week and daily too. Therefore, which price should be taken to know the money value of the product is a question. Besides we see there are different prices in the market like retail price, wholesale price, etc.

Practical Difficulties

Different types of practical difficulties arise in the estimation of national income. More important difficulties are as follows:

1) Non-monetised Sector: A large part of the under developed countries consists of non-monetised sector. It refers to that part of the economy where the exchange transaction are not performed in money or there is a barter system in the non-monetised sector. Goods which do not enter into the monetary sector are excluded from the national income.

2) Lack of Occupational Specialisation: It means that a person performs a number of economic activities at one and the same time. As a result there are different sources of income to him. It becomes impossible to trace out the main source of earning of an individual, In the absence of adequate information a large part of income remains excluded from the national income.

3) Non-availability of Reliable Data: This type of difficulty arises mainly in under developed countries where majority people are illiterate who can not keep income data nor they can maintain records in this respect. Some-times producers intentionally distort their income. Sometimes enumerators do no not possess the knowledge of collecting data, classifying and analyzing the data. They may have personal bias and prejudice also.

4) Goods for Self Consumption: Producers of final good keep a part of their produce for self consumption. For example, a farmer keeps some crop produced by him for his family. Goods which are retained by the producers for personal consumption do not fetch income and therefore, are excluded from the national income.

5) Double Counting : Many goods and services appear more than once in the national income. It is not always possible to make a distinction between intermediate good and final goods. Likewise building, furniture, machine, etc. should form the part of a year's national income or should be continuously included in the national income till they are finally consumed?

GNP Deflator

The GNP deflator measures the average level of prices of all goods and services produced in the economy during an accounting year. GNP deflator is measured as the ratio of nominal GNP to real GNP multiplied by 100. GNP deflator shows the change in GNP because of change in the price level. In other words, GNP deflator refers to the change in price index for GNP.

Like GNP deflator we also have GDP deflator. GDP deflator is measured as the ratio of nominal GDP to real GDP multiplied by 100.

Green GNP

It is suggested that GNP index should account for cost in terms of environmental pollution and cost in terms of excessive exploitation of natural resources to the extent that it reduces the availability of resources for future generation. Estimation of GNP that accounts for such parameters is called the Green GNP.

Limitations of GDP as a measure of welfare

Often GDP is considered as an indicator of welfare of the people. When GDP rises the flow of goods and services tend to rise. This means the more availability of goods per person showing the higher level of welfare of the nation. But there are limitations to this generalisation. Following points are important in this context.

1) If with every increase in GDP, distribution of GDP is getting more unequal welfare of the society may not rise. The gap between rich and poor may increase.

2) There is no increase in the welfare of the common man if GDP has risen due to increase in the production of defense goods.

3) Non-monetary transactions are not recorded in the GDP to this extent GDP is under estimated. Therefore, GDP is not a proper indicator of welfare.

4) Positive or negative impact of externalities is not accounted in the index of social welfare in terms of GDP. To that extent it either underestimates or overestimates the level of welfare.

———————————

QUESTIONS

1. Define National Income
2. What are the methods of measurement of National Income?
3. Explain the Circular Flow of Income.
4. What are the difficulties in measurement of National Income?
5. Write note on following:
   a) Gross National Product
   b) Net National Product
   c) National Income at Factor Cost
   d) National Income at Factor Prices

Chapter 3

MONEY

CONTENTS

INTRODUCTION

Money is an important element in a modern economy. It works like a lubricant which helps to run economy smoothly. We will try to explain the meaning of money and its various functions. In addition to this we are also going to explain classical and Keynesian approach regarding demand for money. Supply of money affects different factors of the economy. Role of Central Bank is important in this regard. Reserve Bank of India uses various measures to know total supply of money in the economy. Credit created by the commercial banks is one of the important constituents of money supply.

3.1 MEANING OF MONEY

Money is anything that is acceptable as a means of payment in the settlement of transactions including debt. Money is commonly used as a medium of exchange. It is the money which enables people to carry out transactions. Even the performance of business units is measured in terms of money. Therefore, the study of money is quite important.

Various things have served as money at different times. They have varied from shells, goats, cows, silver and gold coins, paper notes and coins. At present, in India, money comprises paper currency, coins and demand deposits of banks.

Definition of Money

It is difficult to define money in clear terms because there are several categories of assets which possess the characteristics of money. Hence, different criteria are used by different economists for defining money. Various authors have given different definitions of money. Professor D. H. Robertson defined money as "any thing which is widely accepted in payment for goods or in discharge of other kinds of business obligations."

According to Crowther, "Money can be defined as anything that is generally acceptable as a means of exchange and that at the same time acts as a measure and a store of a value."

Functions of Money

In a modern economy, money performs a large number of functions. These functions may be classified into three categories- i) Primary functions, ii) Secondary functions and iii) Contingent functions. Following are the functions of money :

a) Primary Functions

Economists consider primary functions of money as those functions which are performed irrespective of the time and place. In a sense, these are the basic functions of money. These functions are:

1. Medium of Exchange

The fundamental role of money in an economy is to serve as a medium of exchange or as a means of payment. Money enables people to carry out their transactions smoothly. People can sell their produce in a market and obtain money, which can be used for purchasing other goods or services required by them. In order to be a good medium of exchange money should have the attributes such as uniformity, durability, portability, divisibility and general acceptability. Its durability enables it to play the role of purchasing power and portability makes it convenient for transactions. Its divisibility promotes carrying out transactions smoothly and general acceptability creates public confidence in money.

2. Measure of Value or Unit of Account

The second important function of money is that it serves as a measure of value or a unit of account. As Crowther has pointed out, "Money acts as a yardstick or standard measure of value to which all other things can be compared." Money helps in expressing the value in exchange of various goods and services and thus, gives rise to the price system.

In an economy where huge number of transactions take place, there will be millions of direct value ratios which are difficult to remember by the people. Money enables to express the values of different goods and services correctly. Thus, money provides a language of economic communication and makes the operation of price system or market mechanism to operate smoothly and systematically. Money, thus enables us to measure the aggregate real output of the economy as a national income in terms of money. Money has been described as a revolutionary invention of modern times. Culbertson observes, "Prices quoted in terms of money become the focus of people's behaviour. Their calculations, plans, expectations and contracts focus on money prices."

b) Secondary Functions

The secondary functions of money are also important. Let us discuss them as follows :

1. Store of Value

Money also acts as a store of value. As Stonier and Hague have argued, "The good chosen as money is always something which can be kept for long periods without deterioration or wastage. It is a form in which wealth can be kept intact from one year to the next. Money is a bridge from the present to the future. It is therefore essential that the money commodity should always be one which can be easily and safely stored."

Some economists distinguish between money's function as a temporary abode of the purchasing power and its function as a permanent abode of the purchasing power. As a temporary store of value, its role relates to money as a form of good in which purchasing power is held by individuals and forms for short period to bridge the time gap between income and expenditure. In addition money is also required as a permanent abode of purchasing power. In other words, there is the asset demand for money. Instead of storing all wealth in the form of non liquid assets like land, buildings, shares etc. People prefer to hold a part of their total wealth in the form of liquid asset such as money. This preference for cash over non cash assets flows from the liquidity characteristic of money and uncertainty about future values of non cash assets. As Keynes has observed, "The importance of money essentially flows from its being 'link' between the present and future."

The use of money as a store of value has certain disadvantages. The value of money does not remain stable. When its value deteriorates, the hoarder of money suffers a loss and gains when its value appreciates.

2. Standard of Deferred Payments

Money also acts as a standard of deferred or postponed payments. Money has made possible to take loan and make repayment after some time because the unit of account is durable. Money links the present values with those of future and helps in simplifying transactions. Commodities other than money do not have general acceptability, comparatively stable values, durability and homogeneity; hence they cannot be used for the purpose of deferred payments.

However, there is a change in the value of money over time which may be harmful or beneficial to debtor and creditor. When the value of money rises over time, the creditor gains and the debtor loses. On the other hand, a fall in the value of money over time benefits to debtor and harms to the creditor. In order to overcome this difficulty, some countries, have fixed debt contracts in terms of a price index, so as to guarantee the future payment of debt by compensating the loser by the same amount of purchasing power prevailing at the time of entering into the contract.

3. Transfer of Value

Money is not only the most liquid form of wealth but also has general acceptability as a means of payment and acts as a store of value. Hence, it helps in transferring value from one place to another. It is this characteristic of money which has increased inter-regional mobility of capital in the modern times. Revolution in the means of transport and communications has increased significantly, has increased the importance of money for transferring purchasing power from one place to another. Now a days NEFT and RTGS are extensively used for this purpose.

c) Contingent Functions of Money

In addition to the primary and secondary functions, money also performs certain contingent or incidental functions, especially in modern developed economies. David Kinley has discussed these as follows:

1. Money as the Most Liquid of all Liquid Assets

Money provides the most liquid form of the liquid assets in which wealth may be held by individuals and firms. They may choose any form for holding wealth in terms of current, demand and time deposits, bonds, treasury bills, government securities, debentures, preference shares and ordinary shares, consumer goods, productive equipments etc. As these are liquid forms of wealth, they can be converted into money very easily.

2. Basis of the Credit System

Money provides necessary base for developing credit system in the economy. Credit facilities are provided by the commercial banks to needy people. In other words banks cannot create credit without having sufficient reserves of money with them as primary deposits.

3. Equaliser of Marginal Utilities and Marginal Productivities

Money also acts as an equaliser of marginal utilities for the consumer. A consumer aims at maximising his satisfaction by spending a given sum of money on various goods needed by him. As the prices of goods indicate their marginal utilities and are expressed in terms of money. It may be said that money helps in the process of equalising the marginal utilities of various goods. This calls for equality between the ratios of the marginal utilities and prices of various goods. Similarly, money helps in equalising the marginal productivities of various factors of production. As the producer aims at maximising his profits, he equalises the marginal productivity of each factor with its price. The price of each factor is paid in terms of money.

4. Measurement and Distribution of National Income

Under barter system it was difficult to measure and distribute the national income. But the invention of money has made it possible. Money helps not only in measuring national income of the economy but also in its distribution as the factors of production are paid in terms of money in the form of rent, interest, wages and profits.

5. Gives Generic Value to Capital

On account of uncertain socio-economic environment, it is difficult for investors to predict suitable opportunity in future for profitable investment. Hence, only those investors who keep their capital in the form of money can exploit the opportunity as and when it gets. Those people who keep their capital in the form of real asset like land and building cannot take the advantage of such opportunities as they do not possess the liquid asset like money.

6. Guarantor of Solvency

Banks, trading companies and other commercial organisations have to maintain their creditability by maintaining solvency. So they prefer to keep certain amount of money for meeting their obligations. Failure to keep adequate cash reserve may lead to insolvency for a commercial bank. Hence, these banks should not only have sound assets position but they must have sufficient liquidity in their assets structure. Money holding of the firm thus provide liquidity to its assets structure but also support as the guarantee of liquidity.

These functions of money have been summarised in the following couplet:

"Money is a matter of functions four,
A medium, a measure, a standard, a store."

Classification of Money

On the basis of materials used, money can be classified as commodity money or metallic money and paper money.

a) Metallic money

Money made of any metal like gold, silver, copper, nickel etc. is called metallic money. It can be further classified as follows:

i) Standard Money

According to Chandler, standard money is a money whose value as a commodity for non commodity purposes is as great as its value as money. Thus, the face value of the coin is equal to its intrinsic or metallic value. Hence, the holder of such coins may use them as money or as metal by melting them. Hence, it is called Full-bodied money. In India, the Rupee coin made up of silver during 1835-1893, was a full bodied coin. Standard money is also unlimited legal tender in which any amount of payments can be made.

ii) Token Money

When the intrinsic value of the coin is less than face value, it is called token or representative money. At present, rupee coin in India is a token money because if it is melted the metal value is not equal to one rupee.

iii) Subsidiary Money

Money which assists the token money is called subsidiary money. All coins in India from 1 paisa to 25 paise were subsidiary money. Such coins are limited legal tender because they can be used to make payment up to a certain limit only.

b) Paper Money

Paper money includes currency notes made of paper and issued by the central bank or the government of the country. Paper money can be further classified as follows:

i) Representative Paper Money

According to Chandler, representative paper money is, "in effect a circulating ware house receipt for full bodied coins or their equivalent in bullion." It is called representative full bodied money, because it is fully backed by the gold bullion held by the treasury.

ii) Convertible Paper Money

It is the money which does not have 100 percent support in the form of standard coins or bullion. But the holder of the paper money can get it converted into bullion or coins on demand.

iii) Inconvertible Paper Money or Fiduciary Money

The paper money which does not have backing of standard coins or bullion and is also not convertible into them is called non convertible paper money. At present, notes issued by the central banks of all the countries are inconvertible paper money.

iv) Fiat Money

Paper money which circulates on the authority or fiat of the government is called fiat money. As Keynes has described, fiat money is a token or representative money which is created and issued by the state but is not convertible by law into anything other than itself and has no fixed value in terms of an objective standard. At present, all inconvertible paper money is a fiat money.

c) Money of Account and Money Proper

As Keynes has explained, money of account is that in which debts, prices and general purchasing power are expressed. Money proper, on the other hand is the actual money in which contracts and debts are settled. For example, Indian Rupee, American Dollar, British Pound etc.

Generally, there is no difference between money of account and money proper, when the accounts in a country are maintained in money proper. But, if the accounts are kept in some other currency, then the difference arises. For example, in Germany after the First World War, the money of account was the American Dollar but the money proper was the Mark.

d) Legal Tender Money and Non Legal Tender Money

Keynes classified money on the basis of its legality as follows :

i) Legal Tender Money

It is the money which the state or government and the people accept as a means of payment and for discharging debts. As it is supported by the government authority, such money is accepted compulsorily by all the people. All the currency notes and coins issued by the government and the central bank of the country are compulsory legal tender in that country.

Legal Tender Money is further classified into limited and unlimited legal tender money.

   a) Limited Legal Tender Money includes all coins of denomination of one paisa to 25 paise were limited legal tender money in India because payments made through them could only be made up to a certain limit only.

   b) Unlimited Legal Tender Money : In India, all paper currency notes and coins of 50 paisa and one rupee are unlimited legal tender because people have to accept payments in unlimited quantities in the form of currency notes and 50 paise and one rupee coins.

ii) Non Legal Tender Money

Money which has no legal authority of the state or the central bank of a country is called non legal tender money. Robertson calls it as "Optional Money." For example, bank money in the form of cheque, draft, bill of exchange, promissory note etc. are the examples of non legal tender money. It is not compulsory for the people to accept such money as there is no legal sanction to support them but this is used by the people more often now a days as this is the part of the banking system.

Disadvantages of Money

According to Bible, "The love of money is the root of all evil." The classical economists treated money as a tool which facilitates exchange of commodities. But in modern economics money plays an important role in promoting wealth and welfare of the people. However, money if not managed properly may give rise to disadvantages as discussed below:

1) Instability in the value of money

The main defect of money is that its value does not remain stable over a period of time. The value of money changes with the changes in total supply of money. When the supply of money in the economy increases than the requirement, the value of money falls and price level rises or inflation takes place. On the contrary, when supply of money decreases, the value of money rises and price level falls or deflation takes place. Thus, the changes in the value of money tend to be harmful to the society.

2) Cyclical Fluctuations

Money is also responsible for giving rise to cyclical fluctuations in a capitalist economy. When the supply of money expands, it gives rise to boom which results into increase in employment, output, income and over production. When the supply of money contracts is generates depression in the economy which results into a fall in income, employment and output which leads to a fall in effective demand and fall in the level of consumption. These cyclical fluctuations result into instability in the economy and miseries to the public at large.

3) Unequal Distribution of Income and Wealth

The changes in the value of money give rise to inflation and deflation which benefits to certain groups of people and damages to the other groups of people. As a result unequal distribution of income and wealth takes place. It tends to widen the gap between rich and poor people and may generate social tensions and social conflicts in the society.

4) Non Economic Defects

Money also brings down morality and promotes corruption, malpractices, political bankruptcy, theft, murders etc.

Although, money has contributed significantly towards our material welfare, it has reacted adversely on our total happiness by reducing our non material welfare.

5) The Veil of Money

According to Prof. Pigou, "money is clearly a veil and it makes hardly any difference whether the veil is thick or thin. He argued that monetary facts and happenings differ from real facts and happenings in that, unlike these, they have no direct significance for economic welfare. Take the real facts and happenings away and monetary facts and happenings necessarily vanish with them, but take the money away and whatever else might follow, economic life would not become meaningless - there is nothing absurd about any money at all. In this sense money clearly is a veil. It does not comprise any of the essentials of economic life."

In spite of these limitations, money is being used extensively in modern economies. The defects of money arise only when it is not managed properly. As Robertson has pointed out, "Money which is a source of so many blessings to mankind becomes also, unless we control it a source of peril and confusion."

3.2 DEMAND FOR MONEY – CLASSICAL AND KEYNESIAN APPROACH

Demand for consumer goods arises for direct consumption. Money is demanded not for its own sake but because of the fact that it performs two important functions, namely i.e. the medium of exchange and the store of value. Thus, money is demanded by individuals and business organizations as they wish to hold money partly in the form of cash and partly as an asset. Thus, the demand for money is a derived demand and not a direct demand. The demand for money means the desire of households and firms to hold a portion of assets in the form of money or liquid assets such as coins and currency notes and bank balances of current accounts. Economists have developed different approaches to explain the demand for money.

Classical approach

Prominent Classical economists like David Hume, J. S. Mill, Irving Fisher etc. held that people demand money for transaction purpose. Because, money is a medium of exchange and hence, it is demanded to carry out transactions of goods and services smoothly. Thus, money is demanded for spending and not for hoarding. According to the classical approach demand for money is a flow of money required for the purpose of transactions over a period of time. Under classical approach there are two distinct views about demand for money. These are:

1) Fisher's Transactions Balance Approach and
2) The Cambridge Cash-Balance Approach

Let us discuss them briefly as follows –

Fisher's Transactions Balance Approach

According to Fisher and other classical economists money is demanded by the people for the purpose of transactions which involve purchase of goods and services. According to accounting identity, value paid must be equal to value received. Thus, in a given period, the value of all goods and services sold must be equal to the number of transactions (T) made multiplied by the average price (P) of these transactions. Thus, the total value of transactions made is equal to PT.

The value paid is equal to the value of money flow used for buying goods and services. The value of money flow is given by the nominal quantity of money supply (M) multiplied by the average number of times the quantity of money in circulation is used or exchanged for transaction purposes (V).

Thus, Fisher's equation of exchange is

$$MV = PT$$

Where,   M = Total quantity of money in circulation
          V = Velocity of Money
          P = Price level or Average price
          T = Total number of transactions

Thus, demand for money depends on the three factors –

  i) Number of transactions (T)
  ii) Average price level (P) and
  iii) Velocity of money (V)

In the short period T and V remain constant hence, the demand for money varies directly with the changes in price level. According to Fisher, changes in the price level are directly proportional to the changes in money supply (Ms) in the short period. So,

$$Ms = Md$$

According to Fisher, the demand for money is always equal to the supply of money, when the economy is in monetary equilibrium.

In his approach, the demand for money is defined objectively in mechanical sense and attention is not paid to the motives behind the demand for money. Thus, demand for money is considered as technical requirement and not a behavioural function.

The Cambridge Cash-Balance Approach

The Cambridge Cash-Balance approach to the demand for money was developed by Prof. Marshall and Prof Pigou. Fisher emphasised on the use of money as a medium of exchange but Pigou in his Cash-Balance approach places emphasis on the function of money as a store of value. The function of money as a store of value stresses on holding money as a general purchasing power by individuals over a period of time.

According to Marshall and Pigou, the demand for money is the amount of money that people want to hold or cash balances held by the people. The total demand for money in the economy can be obtained by adding the demand of all the individuals for holding cash balances.

This approach considered choice determined behaviour of the people for analysing demand for money. They also recognized that, certain factors, such as, (i) current interest rate (ii) wealth owned by the individuals (iii) expectations of future prices and

(iv) future rate of interest determine the demand for money. They believed that during short period these factors remain constant.

Thus, they held that, the total demand for money or cash balances is the proportion of the nominal or money income. Hence, aggregate demand for money can be expressed symbolically as follows :

$Md = kPY$

Where,

Md = The demand for money

k = Proportion of nominal income (PY) that people want to hold as cash balances

P = average price level of currently produced goods and services.

Y = real national income

PY = nominal national income

According to this approach

i) The demand for money is a function of money income alone. It makes the relation between demand for money and income as behavioural whereas according to Fisher's approach, demand for money is related to total transactions in a mechanical manner.

ii) According to the Cambridge cash balance approach, the demand for money is proportional function of nominal income ($Md = KPY$). It is a proportional function of both price level (P) and real income (Y). This implies that (i) income elasticity of demand for money is unity and (ii) price elasticity of demand for money is also equal to unity. Hence, any change in the price level causes equal proportionate change in the demand for money.

The Cambridge approach may be considered as superior to the Fisher's approach. However, it has not provided comprehensive and satisfactory explanation about the demand for money. It was Keynes who developed the comprehensive theory of demand for money taking into consideration relationship between money and economic activity in a more satisfactory way.

The Keynesian Approach

Keynesian theory of the demand for money was first formulated by Keynes in his well known book, 'The General Theory of Employment, Interest and Money' (1936). It has been developed further by other economists of Keynesian school.

Keynes developed a theory of demand for money which occupies an important place is the monetary theory. He introduced the new concept of 'Liquidity Preferenc' to explain the demand for money. Liquidity preference means the demand for money is the desire of public to hold cash. He explained the demand for money in terms of motives for liquidity preference. According to Keynes, the desire for liquidity arises on account of three motives: i) the transactions motive; ii) the precautionary motive and iii) the speculative motive.

i) The transactions Motive of Demand for Money

The transactions motive gives rise to the transactions demand for money which refers to the demand for cash of the public for making current transactions. Many people receive their incomes once in a month while expenditure goes on daily basis. So, people prefer to keep certain amount of ready money in hand to make current payments. This amount depends on the size of the individual's income, interval of receiving income and the methods of payments prevailing in the society.

The businessmen and entrepreneurs also have to keep the part of their income in the form cash to purchase raw materials, to pay transportation charges, to pay advances to the workers etc. The amount of money held depends on the turnover of the business. The demand for money for transactions purposes arises mainly because of the function of money as a medium of exchange.

The demand for money is basically a demand for real cash balances. If price level rises more money balances will be held to purchase the same quantity of goods. Keynes believed that the transactions demand for money depends on the real income and it is not influenced by the rate of interest. However, the recent empirical studies undertaken by Tobin and Baumol concluded that at a higher rate of interest individuals and business firms tend to keep less money holdings at each level of income. The transactions demand for money is income dependent and hence, relatively stable because income does not change suddenly.

ii) Precautionary Motive of Demand for Money

Precautionary motive of demand for money refers to the desire of people to hold cash balances to meet unexpected or unforeseen contingencies such as accidents, illness, unemployment, etc. The precautionary motive considers the function of money as a store of value. An individual's precautionary demand for money is income dependent and is relatively stable. Thus, the larger the income of the individual, the larger is the cash balance held for the future unexpected contingencies. The precautionary demand for money being stable is not significantly affected by the interest rates. Although, the precautionary demand for money is income determined and interest inelastic it may change in response to the changes in uncertainty.

iii) The Speculative Motive of Demand for Money

The speculative motive is the demand for idle balances. This motive for holding cash-balances arises due to uncertainty about the future rate of interest or bond prices. The cash held under this motive is used to make speculative gains by dealing in bonds whose prices fluctuate frequently. Bonds include securities and such papers which yield a fixed or a known rate of interest over a period of time. When the bond prices are expected to rise which means that the rate of interest is expected to fall businessmen will buy bond with a view of selling them when their prices actually rises. When bond prices are expected to fall which means the rate of interest is expected to rise then, businessmen tend to sell bonds to avoid capital losses.

According to Keynes, the demand to hold cash balance under speculative motive implies the, "object of securing profit from knowing better than the market." The speculative motive is related to the store of value function of money. Money is held in the form of liquid assets to make speculative gain expecting changes in the value of bonds or other similar assets.

The demand for idle cash balances is inversely related to the rate of interest. It is highly interest elastic. Given the expectations about the changes in the rate of interest in future less money will be held under the speculative motive at a higher current rate of interest and more money will be held under this motive at a lower current rate of interest. The purpose of holding money under this motive is to earn more income. Increase in speculative demand for money represents higher preference for liquidity. It indicates that people prefer money as the most liquid asset than the other assets.

Thus, under speculative motive, demand for money is a decreasing function of the rate of interest. The higher the rate of interest, the lower is the speculative demand for money and vice versa. This can be expressed as:

$$Ls = f(r)$$

Where, Ls is the speculative demand for money, 'r' is the rate of interest.

It can be explained with the help of diagram as follows :

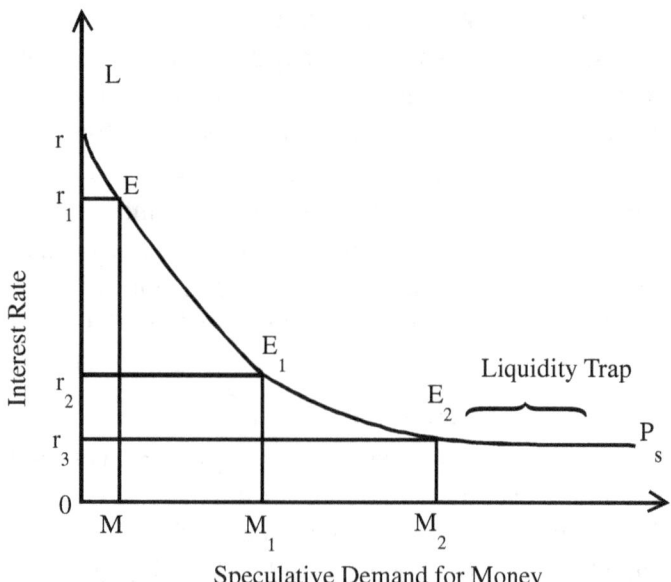

Speculative Demand for Money

The Liquidity Preference curve LP is a downward sloping towards the right signifying that the higher the rate of interest, the lower is the demand for money for speculative motive and vice versa. Thus, at the high current rate of interest a very small amount is held for speculative motive.

The figure shows that, at a very high rate of interest, the speculative demand for money is less. The businessmen prefer to invest all of their cash holdings in bonds as they believe that the interest rate will not rise further. As the interest rate falls to Or_1, the speculative demand for money rises to OM. When the rate of interest falls further to Or_2, the speculative demand for money increases to OM_1. However, at a very low rate of interest such as Or_3, the LP curve becomes perfectly elastic which indicates that the speculative demand for money becomes infinitely elastic. This portion of LP curve is known as 'Liquidity trap'. When the rate of interest is very low, people prefer to hold money in the form of cash rather than investing it in the bonds. Because under such conditions, purchasing bonds means a definite loss. People will wait till interest rate rises to the normal level and bond prices to fall.

Liquidity Trap

The liquidity preference curve LP becomes quite flat means perfectly elastic at a very low rate of interest. It is a horizontal line or parallel to the X axis.

This perfectly elastic portion of liquidity preference curve indicates the position of absolute liquidity preference of the people. It means that at a very low rate of interest people will hold with them as inactive balances any amount of money they come to have. This portion of liquidity preference curve with absolute liquidity preference is called 'liquidity trap' by the economists because expansion in the money supply gets trapped in the sphere of liquidity trap and therefore, cannot affect rate of interest and therefore the level of investment.

According to Keynes, when interest rate is very low, the earnings from bonds are much smaller so, there is more demand for cash holdings.

Implications of Liquidity Trap

i) The monetary authority cannot influence the rate of interest by following a cheap money policy because any increase in the quantity of money cannot lead to a further decline in the rate of interest under liquidity trap situation.

ii) The rate of interest cannot fall to the minimum level zero.

iii) The policy of general wage cut cannot be effective under the conditions characterised by perfectly elastic liquidity preference curve. Such a policy may lead to a lowering wages and prices, but then money released from transactions will be used for speculative purposes and the rate of interest will remain unaffected as people will hold money due to uncertainty prevailing in the money market.

Although, the concept of liquidity trap developed by the Keynes is interesting to study but there is no historical evidence of a situation characterised by a liquidity trap in any country.

Total Demand for Money

The total demand for money depends on –
  a) the transactions and precautionary motives
  b) the speculative motive

According to Keynes, the money demanded for transactions and precautionary motive (M_1) is completely interest inelastic unless interest rate is very high. The amount of money demanded for these motives vary with the level of income or it is a function of size of income. Thus,

$$M_1 = L_1(Y)$$

Where,

M_1 is money demanded or held under transactions and precautionary motive is a function of income.

Y stands for income and
L_1 stands for demand function.

However, money demanded for speculative motive (M_2) is a function of rate of interest.

$$M_2 = L_2(r)$$

Where,
r indicates rate of interest and
L_2 stands for the demand function for speculative purposes.

In practice, the demand for money held under each motive is difficult to identify, hence, total cash balances are regarded as all the factors together relating to these three motives. Thus

$$Md = L_1 + L_2$$

Where,
Md = total demand for money
L_1 = Money held under the transactions and precautionary motives
L_2 = demand for money for speculative motive

Thus, according to Keynes, total demand for money is the demand function with two separate components.

The community's total demand for money depends upon two variables (i) the nominal level of aggregate income (Y) and (ii) the rate of interest (r). This is shown in

the following figure :–

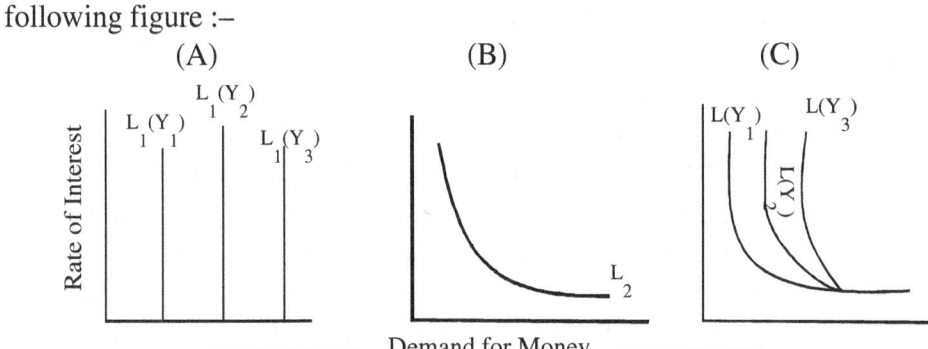

In the figure, panel (A) shows the schedule of active balances held at different levels of income. The demand for active balances is perfectly interest inelastic in the short period and it changes in proportion to the changes in income. The curves $L_1(Y_1)$, $L_1(Y_2)$ and $L_1(Y_3)$ indicate demand for active balances at income levels Y_1, Y_2 and Y_3. As the demand for active balances or for transaction and precautionary motives is interest inelastic these curves are vertical straight lines.

The curve L_2 in the panel (B) of the figure represents the demand for money under speculative motive or idle cash balances which is the inverse function of the rate of interest, so L_2 curve slopes downward and at the minimum level it becomes parallel to the x axis or horizontal.

Panel (C) represents the horizontal summation of curves in panel (A) and (B). Thus, $L(Y_1)$, $L(Y_2)$ and $L(Y_3)$ curves represent the liquidity preference schedule or the total demand for money. It shows that the demand for money varies inversely with the rate of interest and it increases with the increase in national income.

Criticism on Keynesian Approach

The classical theory of demand for money considered only transactions demand for money but Keynes introduced the speculative motive for demand for money. However, Keynes' approach has been criticized on the following grounds:

i) Modern economists have rejected Keynes' additive form of demand for money function on the grounds that money represents a single asset and not several ones. There may be more than one motive to hold money and the same unit of money can serve several motives. Hence, the demand for money cannot be divided into separate compartments independently of each other.

ii) Tobin and Baumol have argued that the transactions demand for money also depends on the rate of interest.

iii) Other economists have explained that speculative demand for money is an increasing function of the total assets or wealth. If income is taken as a proxy of total wealth then speculative demand for money will also depend upon the size of income apart from the rate of interest. So, the total demand for money function may be written in modified form as $Md = L(Y, r)$ where it is held that, the demand for money function (Md) is increasing function of the level of income and a decreasing function of rate of interest. This modified form of demand for money function has been considered as a significant development in the monetary theory.

iv) Under speculative demand for money, it is assumed that people hold their assets in either money or bonds only which is unrealistic as people hold their financial wealth in some combination of both money and bonds. Hence, Tobin, Baumol Friedman etc. have developed the portfolio approach to the demand for money.

In spite of these limitations, we can say that the Keynesian approach has been considered as an important contribution towards the development of monetary theory.

3.3 SUPPLY OF MONEY

Money supply plays an important role in the determination of price level and interest rate. The money supply is determined by the policy of the central bank of a country and the government. The commercial banks also play a crucial role in money supply through credit creation. A money supply is important not only for acceleration of economic growth but also for achieving price stability in the economy. A healthy growth of economy needs that there should be neither inflation nor deflation. It is necessary to keep money supply within limits so that it can accelerate economic growth otherwise it creates inflation which is more harmful for the economy. Therefore, central bank of a country performs the role to control credit so that economy can grow without inflation or deflation.

a) Role of Central Bank - Credit Control

Every country has its own central bank. It is a symbol of financial sovereignty and stability of the country. A central bank is an institution which is responsible for safeguarding the financial stability of the country. It holds the ultimate reserves of the nation, controls the flow of purchasing power - whether currency or credit and acts as a banker to the government.

The importance of central banks has been steadily increasing on account of various reasons. The interdependence of economic life within and between the countries is increasing. The need for management and control of currency system has been significantly increased. In order to control business cycles in developed countries and to promote economic development of developing countries , central banks are playing active role. They also co-ordinate, control and manage various dynamic complicated and conflicting issues which affect economic stability in the national and international field.

Definition of Central Bank

i) According to Shaw, "a central bank is a bank which controls credit."

ii) Hawtrey defines a central bank is that which is the lender of the last resort.

iii) According to Day, a central bank is "to help, control and stabilise the monetary and banking system."

iv) Sayers defined it as, "the organ of government that undertakes the major financial operations of the government and by its conduct and other means influences the behaviour of financial institutions so as to support the economic policy of the Government."

v) Samuelson defined central bank as, "a bank of bankers. Its duty is to control the monetary base and through the control of this high powered money to control the community's supply of money."

The central bank is not a profit making institution. It plays an active role in the economy and it is not subservient to any political party but it acts in the interest of the economy as a whole.

The main objective of a central bank is not to earn profit but to work for the benefit and welfare of the society as a whole. It aims at achieving this objective by way of carrying out the following functions.

Functions of a Central Bank

A central bank performs several functions. However, the main functions are as discussed below.

1) Regulator of Currency and Bank of Issue

The central bank enjoys monopoly of note issue. It not only gives uniformity to the system of note issue but also provides prestige to the currency notes. This Monopoly enables the central bank to exercise control over other banks in the expansion of credit, as it is the cash reserve that determines the limit of such expansion.

2) Banker, Fiscal Agent and Advisor to the Government

A central bank functions as a banker to the government. All balances of the goverment of the country are kept with the central bank.

The central bank also functions as the fiscal agent of the government and advises the Government in the matters relating to currency, exchange and finance. It looks after exchange, remittance and other bank operations including management of public debt. The main reason of a central bank operates as a banker to the state because of closer interrelation between public finance and monetary affairs.

The important function of the central bank relating to the government is the provision of short term loans through discounting the government treasury bills. This enables a government to meet its current financial obligations in anticipation of its revenues.

3) Custodian of the Cash Reserves of Commercial Banks

Commercial banks, according to law, have to keep reserves equal to a certain percentage of both time and demand deposits liabilities with the central bank. Thus, the central banks acts as a custodian of the cash reserves of commercial banks and helps in facilitating transactions of commercial banks.

4) Lender of the Last Resort

When the commercial banks face shortages of financial resources, the central bank serves as a lender of last resort. It acts through its rediscounting operations.

5) Clearing House for Transfer and settlement

Since banks keep cash reserves with the central bank, transfer and settlement of claims between them can be easily carried out by means of debits and credits in the books of the central bank. As the central bank acts as a clearing agency, it is economical and time saving and convenient to commercial banks.

6) Custody and Management of Foreign Exchange Reserves

The central bank keeps and manages the foreign exchange reserves of the country. It always buys and sells foreign currencies at international prices. It also fixes the exchange rates of the domestic currency in terms of foreign currencies. It also manages exchange control operations by supplying foreign currencies to importers, businessmen and students going abroad.

7) Controller of Credit

Controlling credit in the economy is the most important function of the central bank. The controller of credit means the regulation and control of bank advances, bank credit has become an important constituent of the money supply of the country. The volume and direction of bank credit has a significant impact on the level of economic activities in a country. Excessive credit tends to generate inflationary conditions in the economy while deficiency of credit supply may result into depression or deflation. Lack of availability of cheap credit may hinder the process of economic development of a country. Whether it is inflation or deflation, both are harmful to the society. In order, to avoid inflation and deflation or to maintain economic stability and promote economic growth, the central bank has to control credit in the economy.

Objectives of Credit Control

The purpose of credit control exercised by the central bank aims at achieving the following objectives :

1) To eliminate fluctuations in output and employment level
2) To maintain internal price stability
3) To achieve stability in foreign exchange rates
4) To promote economic growth
5) To safeguard gold reserves against internal and external drains.

Thus, the central bank uses credit control as a means to control the lending policy of commercial banks for achieving the objectives stated above.

Difficulties of Credit Control

The central bank has to face several difficulties for achieving efficient credit control. Some of them are discussed below :

i) Bank Credit is a part of total credit activities in the economy. There is also commercial credit like bank credit. The central bank has little control over them. They are as much purchasing power as any other form of credit.

ii) All banks of the country do not have direct relations with the central bank. For example, even in U.S.A one half of the commercial banks with one fifth of resources are outside the Federal Reserve System.

iii) Even if all banks were member banks, commercial banks may not always co-operate with the central bank and may not follow its policy. Such a co-operation is indispensible for a successful credit control.

iv) There are non banking elements in the financial structure of the country which affect the business community but these are beyond the scope of action of the central bank.

v) A central bank cannot control the ultimate use to which credit may be put. For example, commercial loans may be used for speculative purposes.

In spite of these limitation, the central bank of a country which is an apex bank and banker to the government has to take necessary steps to make its credit control successful.

Methods of Credit Control

The central bank uses two types of methods for controlling credit in the economy. These are:

A) Quantitative Methods and

B) Qualitative Methods

Let us discuss these methods.

(A) Quantitative Methods

These methods aim at controlling the cost and volume of credit. These are:

(1) Bank Rate Policy

(2) Open Market Operations

(3) Variable Reserve Ratio

(1) Bank Rate Policy

The bank rate is the rate at which the central bank of a country is willing to discount first class bills.

Bank rate is the interest changed by the central bank. It is fixed by the central bank. By making variations in the bank rate, the central bank controls credit. When it is necessary to expand credit, the central bank lowers the bank rate. Thus, borrowing from the central bank becomes cheaper, so the commercial banks tend to borrow more. As the discount rate on bank rate is lowered, the market rate of interest will also be lowered. The business sector may borrow more funds and business activities tend to increase. As credit expands in the economy prices tend to rise and profits of business also increase.

When the economy needs contraction of credit, the central bank raises the bank rate which increases market rate of interest also. Hence, borrowing from the banks becomes costly. So, the banks as well as the businessmen tend to borrow less. As borrowing becomes costly, new loans are discouraged. Reduction in credit tends to reduce price level in the economy. Thus, raising the bank rate helps central banks to control inflationary tendencies and lowering the bank rate enables them to overcome deflationary tendencies in the economy.

Effects of Variations in the Bank Rate

According to Hawtrey, changes in the bank rate lead to the changes in the short term rates of interest. It influences the willingness of wholesale dealers and middlemen and hence, stocks of finished and partly finished goods will be reduced because these stocks are financed through short term loans. When wholesalers reduce their stocks by placing less orders with producers, the productions in turn gets reduced. As production decreases, employment decreases and hence, incomes of the people and their purchasing power will be reduced. Decrease in purchasing power of the final consumers will affect wholesale dealers adversely. Thus, vicious circle comes into existence in the economy. There is also a psychological effect that people tend to postpone their purchases expecting that prices will fall further. The cumulative effect of all these developments results into depression in the capital goods industries due to less and less orders from the producers.

Conversely, a fall in the bank rate will be followed by the willingness of wholesaler to keep more stocks and they put larger orders with producers which tends to increase employment, output and income in the economy. The sales will be higher, prices tend to rise and profits earned will be more. It stimulates the investment activities in the economy which may lead to increase in production of capital goods industries.

This view is criticized on the grounds that it gives too much importance to the changes in interest rates which is the only one factor in the total costs of holding stocks.

According to Keynes, when the bank rate changes, the long term interest rates also change in the same direction and tend to affect investment, prices, employment and income in the economy.

When bank rate rises it leads to the increase in the short term interest rates in the money market, while long term interest rates remain constant. Hence, short term securities will become more attractive on account of their higher rates of interest. But the value of long term securities falls because they are having lower rates of interest than at which they were purchased earlier. So, the holder of long term securities will sell them and invest in short term securities. Thus, the long term investments in the economy get adversely affected. Consequently, long term rates of interest will tend to increase. So, businessmen and producers will reduce their investments on fixed capital assets. As investments are reduced in capital goods industries, employment and money incomes also decline. The expenditure on consumer goods decreases which results in a fall in their prices and production. Conversely, when the bank rate falls, it will result in a fall in long term interest rates and investment, employment, output, income and prices.

The view of Hawtrey and Keynes have been criticised on the grounds that they cannot be empirically verified and they assume that businessmen and producers are highly sensitive to interest rate changes. This is unrealistic because prices and production are not so sensitive to changes in the interest rates and interest rates form an insignificant part of total cost of production of goods. Although, Hawtrey emphasises on changes in short term interest rates and Keynes on long term interest rates, both arrive at the same conclusion. Both short term and long term rates influence, the general economic situation. In any case they are closely connected.

When bank rate falls, market rate also fall and cost of borrowing from banks becomes cheap. It motivates investors and business firms to obtain more advances from the banks.

Limitations of Bank Rate Policy

Although, the bank rate is considered as an important tool of credit control, it has certain limitations as discussed below :

a) Indirect Weapon

Bank rate is said to be an indirect weapon of credit control because it affects the demand for credit initially and then the supply of credit changes according to the changes in demand. Hence, it is tends to be less effective.

b) Power to Influence the Market Rates -

The efficiency of bank rate policy depends to a great extent on its power to influence the market rates. It requires highly organised money market. Most of the countries do not have well organised money markets. The multiplicity of market rates which are not sensitive to the changes in the bank rate tend to make bank rate policy ineffective. The absence of any type of relationship between the central bank and other components of money market also tend to make bank rate policy ineffective.

c) Ample Excess Reserves with the Banks

If the commercial banks have ample liquid resources at their disposal then there is no need for them to approach the central bank. Hence, bank rate policy may not get expected results.

d) Inelastic Economic Structure

The bank rate policy presupposes an economic system in which the price, wages and interest rates are readily movable and entrepreneurs work on a narrow margin and consequently react very sensitively to the slightest changes in costs and profit. Thus, for a bank rate to be successful, prices wages, costs, production and trade must respond to changes in the bank rate. Such conditions are mostly absent even in the developed countries hence, the bank rate policy tends to be ineffective.

e) Psychological Reactions of Business

During depression businessmen are too much pessimistic and they are not ready to undertake new ventures even if there is considerable fall in interest rates. During a boom period businessmen are optimistic and feel much assured of future profit they may not be ready to reduce their business activities even if there is significant increase in the interest rate.

f) Recent Developments

Several recent developments in the money market have reduced the importance of bank rate policy. Now domestic trade is financed through overdrafts from banks rather than bills of exchange. Foreign bills have lost their importance as the financial status of Londen market has lost its leading role. Now short term treasury bills are being increasingly used in place of bills of exchange. All such changes limits the success of bank rate policy.

Conclusion

Although, the relative importance of the bank rate policy has reduced but it is still in use as an important weapon of credit control. We may conclude that the central bank should rely more on the other instruments also for controlling credit rather than depending only on the bank rate or to make bank rate policy more effective it should be used with other instruments of credit control in combination.

(2) Open Market Operations

The term open market operations implies the purchase and sale of government securities by the central bank. Open market operations became important on account of the limitations of the bank rate policy. It has been observed that open market operations are better suited to influence the market trends directly. In the case of the bank rate policy, the central bank has to wait for the market to react. Thus, its efficiency depends on its indirect influence on the market trends through changes in bank rates whereas open market operations have direct and immediate impact on interest rate and volume of credit. Hence, open market operations are considered more effective and superior than the bank rate policy.

Process of Open Market Operation

The theory of open market operations states that the sale of securities by the central bank leads to the contraction of credit and the purchase of government securities results into expansion of credit in the economy.

When the central bank sells securities in the open market it receives payment from the commercial banks. The cash balance of the bank, reduces to that extent. Due to reduction in its cash the commercial bank has to reduce its lending. As a result credit tends to contract. On the contrary, when the central bank purchases securities it pays through cheques drawn on itself. It results into increase in cash balances of the commercial banks which enables them to expand credit.

The open market operations method is generally used to make bank rate policy more effective. If the member banks do not raise the lending rates after the increase in the bank rate due to surplus funds available with them the central bank can withdraw such surplus funds by way of sale of securities and thus force the member banks to raise their lending rates. Scarcity of funds in the market compels the bank to borrow directly or indirectly from the central bank through rediscounting of bills.

Advantages of Open Market Operations

The open market operations is considered as a very effective weapon of credit control in modern times. Its main advantages may be stated as follows:

a) Direct influence on Market Trends

The open market operations have direct and immediate effect on the volume of credit and interest rates.

b) Complimentary Weapon

In order to make bank rate policy more effective, open market operations can play role as a complementary weapon. Such a combination provides direct and indirect approaches for making credit control policy more effective and successful.

c) Instrument of Public Debt Management

The open market operations serve as useful means for the management of public debt. During the period of inflation, selling of government securities or raising of debt helps in reducing money supply and purchasing power in the economy, so as to bring down the general price level. When there is a depression, the central bank, can purchase the government securities (i.e. repayment of public debt) which tends to increase money supply. Thus, the central bank can maintain price stability in the economy and increase public confidence in the instruments of public debt.

d) Maintaining Balance of Payments Equilibrium

The open market operations also help in maintaining balance of payments equilibrium. During the period of adverse balance of payment situation, the central bank can sell government securities which results into contraction of credit and decrease in the price level in the economy and increase in exports on account of relatively lower prices. During the period of surplus balance the central bank may purchase government securities in open market which will expand money supply and purchasing power in the economy and rise in price level will discourage exports and promote imports.

Limitations of Open Market Operations

The main limitations of open market operations may be stated as follows:

a) Existence of Well Developed Security Market

The success of open market operations depends on the existence of a broad and well developed market for government securities. Lack of well developed security market tends to make open market operations ineffective and unsuccessful.

b) Maintenance of Relatively Stable Cash Ratio by Commercial Banks

If the banks have excess reserve funds then also the policy of open market operations tends to be ineffective.

c) Insensitivity of Commercial Banks

Sometimes the total amount of money in circulation and the cash reserves of the commercial banks may not respond to open market operations of the central bank due to certain disturbing factors. For example, when central bank tries to increase the total amount of money in circulation through purchasing securities certain amount of currency not may be withdrawn for the purpose of hoarding. Conversely, the policy of the central bank to withdraw money from circulation by selling securities may be neutralized by release of notes from hoards.

d) Psychology of Businessmen

The reactions of businessmen also play an important role in determining effectiveness of open market operations. For example, when the central bank adopts the technique of open market operations for increasing the total amount of money in circulation for reviving the general business situation, the businessmen may feel so gloomy and be pessimistic about the future course of prices and profits that they may not be willing to expand their business activities. As DE Kock has pointed out, "Sometimes it is not only a case of unwillingness to borrow on the part of the entrepreneurs, but also the unwillingness to lend, on the part of banks and lenders generally." Thus, on account of risks involved even the banks may not be willing to lend funds.

e) Advantages of Rediscounting Facilities

The banks may neutralize the contraction of credit by making use of the rediscounting facilities provided by the central bank. When commercial banks hold many securities it implies that, their policies regarding commercial loans are insulated from the influence of the central banks' operations.

f) Lack of constant velocity of circulation of Bank Money

The success of open market operations depend upon a constant velocity of credit money. But the velocity of credit money is higher during periods of brisk business activity and lower in the periods of falling prices. Thus, when the velocity of circulation of bank money is higher, the policy of contraction of credit through sale of securities by the central bank may not be successful.

Conclusion

In spite of limitations, open market operations has been considered as an important weapon of credit control at the hands of the central bank. This technique is effectively used in developed countries as they are having active and wider market for short term and long term government securities. However, even developing countries are using it in spite of limitations.

In order to make open market operations policy effective it is necessary that the central bank should take steps to develop active money market and capital market. Bank rate policy and open market operations should be supplemented with other weapons of credit control that are suitable to financial conditions of the country.

(iii) Variable Reserve Ratio

As the traditional weapons of bank rate policy and open market operations were observed to be less effective, the central banks were induced to develop new techniques of credit control. Variable Reserve Ratio or Legal Minimum Requirements as a technique of credit control was first suggested by the Federal Reserve Board of USA in its annual report for 1916, but it was made popular by Keynes in 1930. It was given a permanent status by the Banking Act of 1935 in USA.

Every commercial bank is required by the law to maintain a minimum percentage of its total deposits with the central bank. Whatever amount of money remains with the banks over and above the statutory minimum reserves is called as excess reserves. The commercial banks make use of this excess reserves for creation of credit. Thus, larger the reserve ratio, the lower is the power of a bank to create credit and vice versa. When the central bank wants to expand the credit in the economy then it lowers the reserve ratio say from 25% to 20% so as to increase the credit creation capacity of the commercial banks. The central bank by varying the reserve ratio of the commercial banks influences their power of credit creation and thus controls the credit in the economy.

Objectives of Variable Reserve Ratio

The main objective of variable reserve ratio is to help the central bank with an additional weapon in order to prevent credit expansion or contraction by varying reserve required to be maintained by the commercial banks with the central bank.

Limitation of Variable Reserve Ratio

As a method of credit control, variable reserve ratio has certain limitations.

a) Excess Reserves with the banks

It has been observed that the commercial banks usually possess large excess reserves which tend to make the policy of variable reserve ratio ineffective. When the banks have excess reserves an increase in reserve ratio will not affect their lending operations as they stick to the legal minimum requirements of cash to deposits and can continue to create credit on the basis of excess reserves.

b) Inflexibility of Policy

This policy is inflexible because the minimum reserve ratio fixed by the central bank in uniformally applicable throughout the country. Raising reserve ratio may not be justifiable where there are shortages of money supply although it may desirable for the region where there is excess money supply.

c) Discriminatory in Nature

It affects different banks differently. An increase in reserve ratio may be required for a bank having excess supply but it hits hard to those banks which do not have excess supply. This policy does not affect other financial intermediaries like cooperative societies, insurance companies etc. though they compete with the commercial banks.

d) Business Climate

The success of the policy of the variable reserve ratio depends on psychology of businessmen. For example, during depression businessmen are pessimistic about the future and hence, even significant reduction in the reserve ratio does not encourage the businessmen to borrow. Similarly, during boom period businessmen are highly optimistic about the future hence, substantial increase in the reserve ratio does not discourage them from taking more loans from the banks.

e) Depressive Effect on Securities Market

When the central bank suddenly directs the commercial banks to increase their reserve ratios they may be forced to sell securities to maintain that reserve ratio. This wide spread selling may result in bringing down the prices of securities and may lead to collapse of the bond market.

f) Unsuitable for Day to Day Adjustments

This method cannot be used on the basis of day to day or week to week .

g) Widening of Central Bank's Powers -

The method is criticised on the grounds that it confers upon the central bank very wide powers. But this is not a valid criticism, because the central bank is the institution looking after nation's monetary activities and hence, it must have wide powers. It only implies that these powers should not be used carelessly. So, according to Keynes, the ratio may be varied with due notice and in small degrees.

Conclusion

Despite the limitations the variable reserve ratio has been considered as a useful addition to the armoury of credit control. This method is more useful to countries having under developed money markets where the bank rate policy and open market operation have limited effectiveness.

It may be stated that bank rate policy, open market operations and variable reserve ratio are closely related weapons of credit control. Because, the effect of all these instruments is on the reserve base of banks. Open market operations and variable reserve ratios tend to affect the reserve base directly while the bank rate policy affects indirectly through the cost of reserves. Although, each weapon has a different impact, it is desirable to use all these weapons together for achieving the expected results.

(B) Qualitative Methods of Credit Control

The main objective of qualitative credit controls is to divert bank advances into certain channels or to discourage them from lending for certain purposes. Thus, they affect the use of credit for a particular purpose. These controls have assumed greater importance in modern times. These methods include:

1) Changes in Margin Requirements
2) Regulation of Consumer Credit
3) Rationing of Credit
4) Issue of Directives
5) Direct Action
6) Moral Suasion
7) Publicity

Let us discuss these methods as follows:

1. Changes in Margin Requirements

This technique is used to control excessive use of credit for speculation through buying and selling of securities. The central bank fixes the certain minimum margin requirements on loans for purchasing or holding securities. It is the percentage of the value of security that has to be kept as reserve and it cannot be lent or borrowed. It implies the maximum value of loan which a borrower can borrow from the bank on the basis of security. When the central bank wants to reduce speculative activities it increases the margin requirements and when it wants to expand credit it reduces the margin requirements.

Advantages
  i) It is the more effective technique of controlling inflation as it can be used to control credit in sensitive sectors of the economy where inflation develops rapidly.
  ii) It is the simple and effective technique as it can be used for the use of credit for specific purposes.

2. Regulation of Consumer Credit
   This technique of selective credit control is used to regulate the consumer installment credit and hire purchase finance in developed countries. Substantial part of the credit is used for the consumer durable goods like cars, refrigerators, TVs, computers, two and four wheelers, etc. They are sold on hire purchase or installment credit system. Central bank tries to control such credit in several ways. For example.
   i) by regulating down payment on specific goods.
   ii) by fixing the coverage of durable consumer goods.
   iii) by regulating repayment period of installment credits

Advantages
  i) The regulation of consumer credit is an effective tool of controlling credit in case of durable goods during both slumps and booms where general credit controls are not effective.
  ii) The demand for consumer credit for consumer durables is interest inelastic as consumers buy these goods under the influence of demonstration effect.
  iii) It helps in combating inflation by restricting consumer demand for goods which are in short supply.

Disadvantages
  i) It is technically defective, cumbersome and difficult to administer.
  ii) It discriminates between different types of borrowers and affects only those consumers who have limited income and it does not affect consumers from high income groups.
  iii) In order to make it effective, it has to be used along with other broader, fiscal and other measures of combating inflation.

3) Rationing of Credit
   Credit rationing means restrictions placed by the central bank on demand for credit during times of monetary stringency. The credit is rationed by limiting the amount available to each applicant.

When the demand for credit exceeded the total available resources of the State Bank of Russia. It was obliged to divide the available funds in some definite way among those who needed them. Hence, Russia and Mexico made extensive use of this technique for credit control as these were the planned economies.

There are two ways in which this technique is used.

a) The Variable Portfolio Ceiling

Under this method, the central bank fixes a ceiling on the aggregate portfolios of the commercial banks so that they cannot advance loans beyond this ceiling.

b) The Variable Capital Assets Ratio

Under this method, the central bank fixes the ratio in relation to the capital of commercial bank to its total assets. Depending upon the economic conditions in the economy, the central bank may raise or lower the portfolio ceiling and also may vary the capital assets ratio.

The main disadvantages of this technique are as follows.

This technique involves discrimination against larger banks because it restricts their lending power more than that of the smaller banks.

On account of these limitations the central banks in mixed economies do not use it except under in extreme inflationary conditions and emergencies. But in case of planned or socialist economies it is used quite often for regulating the credit.

4) Issue of Directives

Recently, the central banks have started issuing directives to the commercial banks. However, their effectiveness depends on the status and prestige of the central bank on one hand and the structure of the banking that exists in the economy. These directives are given in the form of oral or written statements, declarations in the newspapers, appeals and warnings for controlling individual credit structure and to restrain the aggregate volume of loans.

Generally, it is observed that on account of increasing competitive pressures commercial banks tend to neglect the directives issued by the central banks for controlling their credit activities. Hence, directives are used as supplementary to the more effective traditional method of credit control.

5) Direct Action

A central bank may adopt the technique of direct action against the commercial banks, which fails to follow the directions given by the central bank. Following are the ways of Direct Action:

i) The central bank may refuse rediscounting facilities to those commercial banks which may be granting too much credit for speculative and unproductive purposes or in excess of their capital and reserves.

ii) The central bank may restraint them from granting advances against the collateral of certain commodities.

iii) It may charge a penal rate of interest from those banks which want to borrow from it beyond the prescribed limit.

iv) It may threaten a bank to be taken over by it if it fails to follow its policies and instructions.

However, direct action gives rise to a situation of conflict when the central bank refuse credit to the commercial banks as a lender of the last resort.

6) Moral Suasion

Moral suasion implies the persuading the commercial banks by the central bank to cooperate with it in following a proper credit policy. The executive head of the central bank calls a meeting of the head of the commercial banks and during the meeting he explains the need of adopting a particular monetary policy under prevailing economic condition and appeals them to co-operate with central bank.

This method tends to be effective in small countries where there are few leading commercial banks and all are the members of the central bank. Hence, the central bank is able to play a role of big brother.

However, the success of this method depends on willingness of commercial banks to follow the central bank; this in turn depends on the strength of the central bank and the status and prestige it commands among the member banks in the country. The technical means and statutory powers at the disposal of the central bank, the degree of co-operation between the central bank and the commercial banks and the nature of country's banking and credit structure. If the banks have excess reserves they may not follow the advice of the central bank. It may not be successful during booms and slumps when the climate of optimism and pessimism plays a dominant role in the economy.

7) Publicity

The central bank may employ the method of publicity in order to make known to the public about its views and to combat opposition to its policies among political, financial and business sections. Generally, the warnings are addressed to the public or to the banks along with the publication of statistical data and statements through popular media.

In order to be successful it calls for educated and knowledgeable public about monetary phenomena. But even in developed countries such percentage of population is much less. Hence, it is doubtful if they can exert moral pressure on the banks for strictly following the policies of the central bank. Thus, this method of selective credit control cannot play a significant role in developing countries.

Limitations of Selective Credit Control

The main limitations of selective credit controls are as follows :

1. Limited to Bank Advances Only

The selective credit controls are concerned with bank advances only and the sources of finances are not controlled by them. For example, borrowing from non banking institutions such as insurance companies, etc. Several companies have reserve funds and undistributed profits at their disposal or they can issue capital or debentures to raise necessary funds.

2. Diversion of Loans

It is possible that the loans taken for other purpose may be used for those activities which are forbidden under the selective credit controls. It is not possible to control the utilisation of bank advances.

3. Bank Lending under Different Labels

The banks lend money under different labels without understanding their customers that they can invest them in forbidden uses. A collusion between banks and their customers tend to defeat the purpose of selective control.

4. Difficulties faced by the Banks

It may be difficult for the central bank to distinguish clearly between essential and non essential sectors and also between speculative and productive investment while enforcing selective control measures. Similar difficulties are also faced by commercial banks for advancing loans.

5. Difficulties in Monitoring Accounts of Commercial Banks

In order to earn maximum profit, the commercial banks may advance loans for forbidden purposes. It is difficult for the central bank to check accounts of commercial banks continuously. Hence, selective credit controls tend to be ineffective.

6. Discrimination among Borrowers

Selective credit controls not only restrict freedom of borrowers and lenders but also discriminates between different types of customers and banks. These controls tend to provide more harm to small banks and small borrowers as compared to the large banks and big borrowers.

7. Misallocation of Resources

Selective credit controls tend to result into misallocation of resources. When they are applied to particular sectors, industries or areas while others are free to operate without such controls.

Conclusion

In spite of limitations the selective credit controls are used by the modern central banks. Instead of depending only on these measures banks make use of them as "second line of instrument." The important point is not the question of general verses selective credit controls, the assessment of the pros and cons as between the two methods, but that of integrating them. Indeed the coordination of selective and general controls appears to have been more effective than the use of any one of them singly.

Role of a Central Bank in a Developing Economy

The main objective of a central bank is to promote economic development of a country at the highest possible rate of growth and maintain rising trends of output, employment and income level in the economy. The main functions of the central bank aimed at achieving these objectives are as follows:

Development of Financial Institutions

In underdeveloped countries commercial banks and financial institutions are not well developed. Hence, voluntary savings are used unproductively and credit facilities are not available for the development of industrial and service sectors. Even the infrastructural facilities are not available for the development of industry and service sector. Even the infrastructural facilities are not developed because of shortage of credit facilities. Hence, the central bank aims at developing a network of banking system and other financial institutions to provide credit facilities in urban and rural areas. It provides incentives to the co-operative sector for developing co-operative societies to serve financial needs of rural populations.

Maintaining Balance between Demand and Supply of Money

The central bank has to play an important role in achieving and maintaining proper balance between the demand and supply of money because any imbalance between supply and demand for money affects the price level adversely. If there is shortage of money it will reduce growth rate of the economy and if there is excess supply of money it results into inflation. For the purpose of promoting economic development supply of money should increase at a higher rate than the demand for money and duo care has to be taken to see that money is not used for financing speculative activities. The central bank has to use monetary policy for controlling uses of money and credit in undesirable channels. It has to use various measures of credit control to achieve the objective of attaining high economic growth rate.

Maintaining Balance of Payments Equilibrium

Developing countries need more imports for which demand is inelastic to promote economic development while for the purpose of export they have only primary products and minerals for which there is elastic demand. As a result, there is a problem of adverse balance of payment. Hence, the central bank has to manage and control the foreign exchange of the country and advice the government on foreign exchange policy. It has to maintain stability in the foreign exchange policy. It has to maintain stability in the foreign exchange rates through exchange controls and bank rate policy.

Promoting Rural Development

As majority of the population resides in rural areas which has to depend on agriculture, hence, the central bank has to take initiative in developing rural banking network and allowing them to give loans on concessional terms to rural industrialists, artisans and craftsmen. In the absence of rural development, urbanisation is taking place at a higher pace which results into congestion in cities and overburdening of the urban services. If rural industries develop rapidly then rural population can get jobs in rural areas and rural migration to urban areas may reduce. The central bank being the apex bank of the country has to take steps to develop credit facilities wherever they are required and promote utilisation of credit for productive purposes.

Even today agriculturists have to depend on local money lenders and relatives for raising loans for agricultural purposes. Development of co-operative societies on sound lines is necesary to provide credit facilities for needy farmers.

Thus, a central bank can play a key role in promoting economic development of the developing countries.

Money and Near Money

In modern economies money has taken different forms ranging from currency notes and coins to bank deposits, cheques, bonds, securities, debentures, treasury bills etc. as they perform some functions of money. However, economists distinguish between money and near money.

Money constitutes those items which have highest liquidity such as currency and demand deposits with the banks, cheques and bank drafts. Because, they perform the functions of money as a medium of exchange.

Those assets which serve as a medium of exchange may be called as money while the assets which serve as a store of value function of money are called the near money.

Near money includes:
  i) Time deposits with banks.
 ii) Bonds, securities, debentures, bills of exchange, treasury bills, insurance policies etc.
iii) Financial companies providing funds on the security of some assets
 iv) Brokers who buy and sell property, bonds, shares, debentures etc. They help in increasing liquidity of these assets by converting them into near money.

According to Hart, people prefer near money to cash because it serves as a margin of safety motive.

Prof Dean points out that, people prefer near money because it gives some returns. Time deposits have higher rate of interest than demand deposits. Time deposits are safer than cash. Banks also encourage savings in near money in order to expand their activities.

The concept of money and near money will be more clear with the help of the table.

Money	Near Money
i) It is a legal tender	i) It has no legal status
ii) It gives liquidity in hand to the possessor	ii) It has liquidity but not ready liquidity.
iii) It performs the function of medium of exchange, a unit of account	iii) It is perfect substitute for money as store of value
iv) Prices are expressed in terms of money.	iv) It is superior to money as it yields income.
	v) It economies use of money properly.
	vi) It helps in reducing quantity of money used by the people.

b) Reserve Bank of India's New Money Measures

RBI classifies factors determining supply of money according to the following categories:

    a) Government borrowing from the banking system.
    b) Borrowing of the private and commercial sector from the banking system.
    c) Changes in net foreign assets held by the RBI caused by changes in balance of payments position and
    d) Government's currency liabilities to the public.

Let us discuss these items briefly :

a) Bank Credit to Government

When government expenditure exceeds government revenue there is a deficit in the government budget so government borrows from the RBI which prints new currency notes for financing it. This process is known as monetisation of deficit or deficit financing. Since 1995 a larger part of budget deficit is financed by the RBI through open market operations by selling government securities to the banks.

The government also borrows from the commercial banks but it results into creation of credit. It increases the money supply in the economy.

b) Bank Credit to the Private and Commercial Sectors

The private sector also borrows from banks whenever their financial resources fall short of their requirements. When commercial bank lend money they create credit which adds to the existing supply of money.

c) Changes in Net Foreign Exchange Assets

Changes in the foreign exchange assets held by the RBI also result in changes in money supply. When there is adverse balance of payment situation, the RBI has to dispose some of its foreign exchange assets. It results in flow of rupees to RBI which pays out foreign exchange. Thus, the high powered money or Reserve Money will be reduced, which leads to decrease in the money supply in the economy. When there is a net surplus in the balance of payment, it results in increase in money supply in the country.

If foreign exchange reserves are used for imports of scarce goods, it helps in reducing inflationary conditions in the economy. Because it tends to reduce money supply that tends to reduce inflation by lowering effective demand and it also results in increase in supply of goods in the economy which tends to reduce prices.

d) Government's Current Liabilities to the Public

Whenever government's currency liabilities increase in terms of coins and one rupee notes, the money supply also increases in the economy.

The Reserve Bank of India has adopted the four concepts of money supply for the purpose of analysis of the quantity and variations in the money supply since April 1977.These measures are discussed below:

(1) M_1 or Narrow Money

It is a narrow measure of money supply which is composed of three items.

$$M_1 = C + DD + OD$$

where,

C = Currency with the public which includes coins, currency notes, cash reserves on hand with all banks.

DD = Demand deposits with the public in commercial and co-operative banks.

OD = Other deposits held by the public with the RBI.

(2) M_2

M_2 is a broader concept of money supply than M_1

$M_2 = M_1$ + post office savings bank deposits.

M_2 has been distinguished from M_1 because saving deposits with post office savings banks are not as liquid as demand deposits with commercial banks as they are not chequeable accounts. However, saving deposits with post offices are more liquid than time deposits with the banks.

(3) M_3 or Broad Money

$M_3 = M_1$ + Time Deposits with commercial and co-operative banks.

M_3 is a broad concept of money supply than M_1 because it includes time deposits with the banks. It is generally believed that time deposits serve as a store of value and are not liquid because they cannot be withdrawn by using cheques. But they may be used for obtaining loans against them from banks whenever needed.

They can also be withdrawn at any time before the due date by forgoing part of interest earned on them.

M_3 has become a popular measure of money supply and it is extensively used by the RBI for its analysis of growth of money supply and its effects on the economy. M_3 is called Aggregate Monetary Resources (AMR).

(4) M_4

The measure M_4 of money supply includes M_3 + total post office deposits.

Reserve bank of India's New Money Measures

The Working Group under the chairmanship of Dr. Y. V. Reddy has suggested major charges in money supply measures. This Working Group was constituted in December 1997, which submitted its recommendations to RBI on June, 1998. The Group suggested four **new money measures** M_0, M_1, M_2 and M_3 and **three liquidity measures** L_1, L_2, and L_3. Besides, the Group also recommended the publishing of financial sector survey after every three months to capture the linkages between banks and rest of the organised financial sector.

Monetary Aggregates

M_0 = Currency in circulation + Bankers deposits with the
RBI + 'Other' Deposits with the RBI.

M_1 = Currency with the Public + Demand Deposits with the Banking System + 'Other' deposits with the RBI = Currency with the public + current deposits with the banking system + Demand Liabilities portion of savings deposits with the banking system + other deposits with the RBI.

M_2 = M_1 + Time liabilities portion of savings deposits with the banking system + Certificate of Deposits issued by Banks + Term Deposits = Currency with the public + Current Deposits with the banking system + term deposits with a maturity up to and including one year with the banking system; and

M_3 = M_2 + Term deposits with a maturity of over one year with the banking system + Call borrowings from 'Non Depository' Financial Corporations by the Banking Systems.

Liquidity Aggregates

L_1 = M_3 + all deposits with the Post Office Savings Banks
(excluding National Savings Certificates)

L_2 = L_1 + Term Deposits with Term Lending Institutions and
Refinancing Institutions (FIs) + Term Borrowing by FIs
+ Certificates of Deposit issued by FIs and

L_3 = L_2 + Public Deposits of Non-Banking Financial Companies.

3.4 ROLE OF COMMERCIAL BANKS - PROCESS OF MULTIPLE CREDIT CREATION AND ITS LIMITATIONS

The creation of credit is one of the important functions of commercial banks. Banks accept deposits from the public and lend money to its customers. When a bank advances loan, it does not pay the amount in cash. But it opens an account in his name and allows him to withdraw the required amount by cheque. In this way a bank creates credit which is regarded as money which can be used for the purchase of goods and services and also for the payment of debt.

Bank deposits arise in two ways:

i) **Primary Deposits**: When a person deposits money with the bank, it is credited in his account. It is a debt of a bank and it has an obligation to repay whenever demanded. This type of deposit is known as primary deposit.

ii) **Derivative Deposits**: Using cash received from the depositors, the banks grant advances to borrowers. Whenever bank grants a loan it does not usually pay cash for it. Instead of paying the cash the banker actually places the amount of loan in the account of the borrower. These deposits are derived from the primary deposits and hence they are known as derivative deposit.

If the banker has more primary deposit, he can lend more and create more credit.

By experience banks know that all depositors do not withdraw their money simultaneously. Some withdraw while some others deposit on the same day. So by keeping a small cash reserves for day to day transactions the bank is able to give loans on the basis of excess reserves. The amount lent may come back again to the same bank or some other bank as deposit. The banks whose deposits have increased will lend. This process will continue till the total deposits have increased by a number of times the original deposit of cash.

Multiple Creation of Credit

The banks have different methods of credit creation.

Loans and Advances: When a loan is granted, the amount of loan is entered in the account of the customer and he is allowed to draw cheques upto the loan amount.

Money at Call and Short Notice: It is given to speculators and stock brokers for very short period. The bank credits the accounts of the stock brokers and allows them to draw the amount.

Discounting of Bills: When a bank discounts a bill of exchange of a customer for a short period of 90 days, the amount of the bill is credited in the account of the customer who withdraws it through cheque.

Investments: A commercial bank also creates a deposit by making investment in securities like shares, bonds, debentures etc. The bank pays for this through a cheque on itself.

The process of credit creation is based on the following assumptions:

i) There are four banks in the banking system.

ii) The required cash reserve ratio for all the banks is 20 percent..

iii) The loan amount drawn by a customer of one bank is deposited in full in the second bank and that of the second bank into the third bank and so on.

iv) Each bank starts with the initial deposit that is deposited by the debtor of the other bank.

Let us see the hypothetical process of credit creation by commercial banks.
On a day the Balance Sheet of the Bank 'A' appears as follows:

Balance Sheet of Bank 'A'

Liabilities		Assets	
Deposits	5000	Cash	5000
	5000		5000

Next day one Mr. Y deposits Rs.5000 with the bank. The balance sheet of the bank after the new deposit of Rs. 5000 is made would be as follows:

Balance Sheet of Bank 'A'

Liabilities		Assets	
Deposits	10000	Cash	10000
	10000		10000

The deposit of Rs. 10000 is a liability to the bank and it has an obligation to repay whenever demanded. This is also an asset because the bank lend or invest to earn income, but after keeping reserve.

Another day, Mr. Z comes with application for a loan of Rs. 8000 to buy a machine. The loan is given. Now the Balance Sheet would appear as follows:

Balance Sheet of Bank 'B'

Liabilities		Assets	
Deposits	10000	Cash	2000
		Loan	8000
	10000		10000

Mr.Z has the right to withdraw upto Rs. 8000. Let us extend our chain of transactions. Supposing Mr. Z issues a cheque for Rs. 8000 to Rajesh & Co. toward buying a machine. Rajesh & Co. deposits the cheque with its Bank 'B'. Bank 'B' will collect the amount from Bank 'A'. After the cheque is collected, the balance sheet of the bank would be as follows:

Balance Sheet of Bank 'B'

Liabilities		Assets	
Deposits	8000	Cash	8000
	8000		8000

Bank 'B' has an excess of Rs. 6400 after keeping 20 per cent reserve, which it can lend or invest. Let us further assume that the bank buys securities of Rs. 6400 from Mr. J. After this transaction, the balance sheet of Bank 'B' would be:

Balance Sheet of Bank 'B'

Liabilities		Assets	
Deposits	8000	Cash	1600
		Investment	6400
	8000		8000

The Bank 'B' may give a cheque for Rs.6400 to Mr. J which may be deposited in his bank or the account of Mr. J will be credited with Rs. 6400 which he may draw at any time.

In our example, the initial cash of Rs. 10000 has created a loan of Rs. 8000, which has become a deposit in another bank. The new deposit has generated another deposit of Rs. 6400 and this process would continue till the original deposit is exhausted completely.

The final sum would be arrived at as following:

Rs. 10000 + 8000 + 6400 + 5120 + ……….. = Rs. 50000

Thus Rs.10000 cash is able to create a new deposit of Rs. 50000. In this way the deposits becomes a loan or investment and in turn becomes a new deposit and it goes on.

This is the process of multiple credit creation by commercial banks.

Deposit Multiplier

The formula for deposit multiplier is:

$$K = 1/r$$

K = Deposit multiplier

r = Ratio Cash Reserve

If the ratio is 20 % or .2. The deposit multiplier is:

$$K = 1/r \text{ i e } 1/.2 = 5$$

If the cash reserve ratio is 10% or .1, the deposit multiplier is 10.

Thus the creation of credit depends upon the ratio of cash reserve to deposit. The higher the cash reserve ratio, the lower will be the credit creation or deposit multiplier.

Limitations on the power of banks to create credit

Banking system as a whole can create credit by way of creating new deposits but there are certain limitations too on the power of commercial banks to create credit.

1. Amount of Cash

The capacity of commercial banks to create credit depends on the availability of cash with them. The larger the amount of cash available with the bank, larger will be the excess funds and hence, larger will be the credit capacity of the banks. As Crowther has observed, "The bank's cash is the lever with which the whole gigantic system is manipulated." The amount of cash which banks have cannot be determined by them. It depends on the primary deposits with the banks.

2. Availability of Collateral Securities

A bank advances loans to its customers on the basis of securities. Banks can create more credit if more securities are available to them and vice versa. As pointed out by Crowther, "The bank does not create money out of thin air, it transmits other forms of wealth into money."

3. Cash Reserve Ratio

The cash reserve ratio fixed by the central bank is an important factor which determines the power of commercial banks to create credit. The higher the reserve ratio, lower will be the capacity of banks to create credit and vice versa.

4. Banking habits of the people

The banking habits of the people also affect the credit creation power of the banks. If the people do not have habit to deposit savings in the banks, use of cheques for the transactions then the loans sanctioned by the banks will be withdrawn in cash as a result credit creation cannot continue and therefore credit creation will be limited.

5. Excess reserves

If the banks prefer to keep excess reserves more than the legal requirements then also the power of banks to create credit will be reduced.

6. Leakages

If there are leakages in the credit creation then also credit creation of banking system will not reach to the maximum level. For example, if some persons who receive cheques may not deposit them in their bank accounts but withdraw money in cash for spending or hoarding. As a result credit expansion cannot take place to the desired level as it will reduce banks capacity to create credit.

7. Behaviour of other banks

If some of the banks do not advance loans to the possible extent then the credit creation process cannot reach to the maximum and the banking system will not be fully loaned up.

8. Economic Climate

During period of boom people tend to borrow more funds from banks on account of favourable investment climate and optimism so credit tends to expand rapidly. But during depression business activities are at the lowest level so businessmen do not eager to borrow funds from the banks. Banks cannot force them to take loans. Hence, credit creation power of banks depend on economic climate in the country.

9. Credit control policy of the Central Bank

The central bank influences the credit creation capacity of the commercial banks. Dear money policy restricts the credit creation capacity of the banks and cheap money policy helps to have more credit creation by the commercial banks.

Thus, it may conclude that commercial banks do not have unlimited power to create credit as there are several factors which affect the credit creation power of the commercial banks.

_____

QUESTIONS

1. Define Money.
2. What are the functions of Money?
3. Explain the classical approach of Demand for Money?
4. Discuss the Keynesian Approach of Demand for Money.
5. Describe the process of multiple credit creation by commercial banks?
6. What are the limitations to the power of banks to create credit?
7. Explain the new money measures of RBI.
8. What are the different methods of credit control?

Chapter 4

VALUE OF MONEY

CONTENTS

INTRODUCTION

The value of money means the purchasing power money over goods and services in a country. What a rupee can buy in India represents the value of money of the rupee. Hence 'Value of Money' is a relative concept which expresses the relationship between a unit of money and the goods and services which can be purchased with it.

The quantity theory of money explains the value of money or price level in terms of changes in the quantity of money in the economy. Classical economist like David Ricardo, J. S. Mill and David Hume explained the value of money in terms of the quantity theory of money. The transaction approach of quantity theory of money is generally associated with the name of Fisher and Cash Balance Approach is associated with the names of Pigou, Marshall and Keynes.

In macro economics the problem of value of money attains vital importance. The value of money is related to the price level because goods and services are purchased with a money unit at given prices. The value of money is of two types: The internal value of money and the external value of money. The internal value of money refers to the purchasing power of money over domestic goods and services. The external value of money refers to the purchasing power of money over foreign goods and services.

4.1 MEANING AND CONCEPT OF VALUE OF MONEY

The value of money means the purchasing power of money over goods and services in a country. What a rupee can buy in India represents the value of money of the rupee. Thus, the value of money expresses the relationship between a unit of money and the goods and services. This shows that the value of money depends on the level of prices. Higher the price level, lower is the value of money and vice versa. Thus, the value of money is inversely related to the price level. Symbolically, it can be expressed as:

$Vm = f(P)$

Where,

Vm stands for value of money and
P stands for price level

The value of money is of two types: The internal value of money and the external value of money. The internal value of money refers to the purchasing power of money over domestic goods and services. The external value of money refers to the purchasing power of money over foreign goods and services.

4.2 QUANTITY THEORY OF MONEY

Prof. Irving Fisher tried to provide formalistic expression to the direct relationship between the quantity of money supply and the general level of prices with the help of the equation of exchange. According to Fisher, the greater the quantity of money, the higher the level of price and vice versa. In other words, the general price level varies directly with the quantity of money or supply of money. Thus, if money supply doubles, prices will also double. If the money supply is reduced to the half then the prices will also get reduced by half.

Equation of Exchange

Fisher has stated a monetary equilibrium as follows:

$MV = PT$

Where,

M stands for total quantity of money
V for the velocity of circulation of money
P stands for the general price level
T refers to the total volume of transactions of goods and services

Thus, MV gives the aggregate effective supply of money or the total money expenditure during a given period.

PT stands for the money value of the things purchased during a given period. Thus, it gives the total demand for money.

Thus, MV = PT shows that under monetary equilibrium, the supply of money is equal to the demand for money.

Fisher's Explanation of Quantity Theory of Money

On the basis of the equation of exchange MV = PT Fisher concluded that, it is the quantity of money (M) that determines the price level (P). The price level (P) varies directly in proportion to the change in the stock of money assuming V and T to be constant.

Initially in this equation only currency money was taken into consideration. Now in the modern economy money includes bank money too. Hence, Fisher extended his equation of exchange to include the bank money. The modified equation may be stated as follows:

PT = MV+M'V'

Where,

        M represents the quantity of money in circulation.
        V = The velocity of circulation of money
        M' = The volume of bank money
        V' = The velocity of circulation of bank money
        T = The volume of transactions during a given period

The equation also indicates that the price level P is directly related to M, M',V, V'and is inversely related to T.

The approach to the determination of value of money adopted by Fisher emphasises proportionality between the changes in the money supply and the changes in the general price level. It can be explained with the help of following figure.

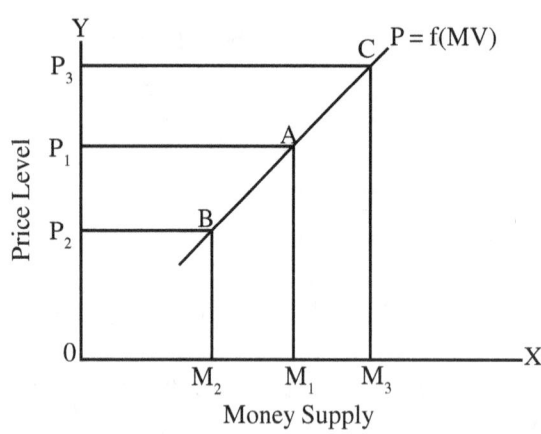

From the figure it is clear that, the curve P is linear, which indicates that the price level varies proportionately to money supply. When the money supply is OM_1, the price level would be OP_1. If the money suply or quantity of money increases to OM_3, the general price level rises to OP_3. In other words, when quantity of money increases by M_1M_3, the general price level increases by P_1P_3 which is an equal rise.

Thus, in response to an increase in the quantity of money the general price level rises proportionately. Similarly, when the quantity of money decreases from OM_1 to OM_2, the general price level falls from OP_1 to OP_2. Thus, the decrease in money supply by M_1M_2 leads to the proportionate fall in price level by P_1P_2.

Thus, Fisher put forth the fundamental thesis which aims to establish, with the help of the equations of exchange that the price level and the value of money is a function of quantity of money only. By way of establishing correlation between the general price level and the quantity of money, he made his equation as an important tool of analysis.

Assumptions of Quantity Theory of Money

Fisher's theory is based on the following assumptions:

1. Price Level (P) is a passive variable. It implies that P does not change automatically. Thus, an increase in M or V only will raise the price level.
2. The ratio M to M' is constant. The quantity of bank money (M') depends on the credit creation activities of commercial banks which depends on the currency money (M).
3. V and V' are assumed to be constant and are independent of changes in M and M'.
4. T also remains constant and is independent of other factors like M, M', V, V'.
5. The Demand for money is proportional to the value of transactions.
6. The supply of money is assumed as an exogenously determined constant.
7. The theory is applicable in the long run.
8. It is based on full employment in the economy.

Criticism of Quantity Theory of Money

Fisher's approach has been criticised on the following grounds

i) The assumption of full employment is unrealistic

Keynes has argued that full employment is a rare phenomenon in a modern economy. When there are unemployed resources in the economy, changes in M may not affect P as T also changes. Under the conditions of unemployment, any increase in the money supply would lead to increase in real income or output. Thus, Fisher's equation does not hold good under the state of unemployment.

ii) The equation of exchange is just a mathematical truism

The equation of exchange does not provide any analytical clue to the determinants of the value of money. It is just a mathematical identity, MV = PT which states that the turnover of money is always equal to the turnover of goods or the money paid is equal to money received. Thus, the cash transactions equation is merely a self evident proposition.

iii) The price level (P) is not a passive factor

The price level (P) is not a passive factor as assumed by Fisher. In practice P is observed to be an active factor. For example P can influence T, because increase in prices leads to higher profits and tend to expand business activities so that T may increase. Rise in P stimulates volume of trade which may lead to an increase in the quantity of money and also in V.

iv) The velocity of circulations of money (V) may not be constant

Fisher as assumed that V is independent and constant which is not correct. It is observed in practice that V varies with the volume of trade and price level. Even actual and expected changes in M also affect V.

v) The equation of exchange has technical inconsistency

In the equation M and V are used, where M refers to money at a given point of time, whereas V refers to the velocity of circulation over a period of time. Under such conditions M and V involves inconsistency of multiplying two non comparable factors.

vi) Fisher's approach is mechanical and it neglects human aspect

According to Fisher, the price level can be controlled by regulating the variables included in the equation. Hence, it is a mechanical explanation. It does not consider effects of decisions of consumers and producers about saving and investment. As money has no will of its own, there is no guarantee that when money supply increases, the expenditure also increases. The fact is that it is the level of expenditure that determines the price level.

vii) Fisher's Approach is one sided

His approach concentrates on the supply side of money as more effective and demand for money is assumed to be constant. Hence, the forces of demand causing changes in the value of money are neglected completely. It considers money as a medium of exchange and neglects store function of money. Thus, factors affecting demand for money are not taken into consideration.

viii) The approach neglects the role of interest rate

According to Mrs. Robinson, the relation between the quantity of money and the price level is not direct. An increase in the supply of money reduces the interest rate which would encourage investment expenditure which along with consumption expenditure tends to determine the price level.

ix) Theoretical dichotomy into theory of money and the theory value

According to Keynes the equation MV = PT artificially divorces the theory of money from the general theory of value. There cannot be a separate theory for explaining the value of money other than the one which explains prices in terms of conditions of demand and supply.

x) Fisher's Approach is Static

His analysis relates to a point of time hence, it is not applicable to modern dynamic conditions.

xi) The ultimate determinants of the value of money lie behind the equation of exchange and not in it.

Chandler has pointed out that, though MV and T are assumed to be immediate determinants of the price level they are not its ultimate determinants but they are determined by a number of underlying objective facts and human decisions.

xii) Failure to make use of the real balance effect

Don Patinkin has criticised Fisher's approach for neglecting the use the real balance effect i.e. the real value of cash balances. A fall in the price level raises the real value of cash balances, which leads to increased spending and hence to rise in income, output and employment in the economy. Fisher has given undue importance to the quantity of money and has neglected the role of real money balances.

xiii) Fisher's approach is of little help in explaining the price movements during various phases of a trade cycle

In spite of these limitations, Fisher's approach has provided foundation for developing other theories related to the value of money.

4.3 THE CASH-BALANCE APPROACH

Cambridge economists, Marshall, Pigou, Robertson and Keynes formulated the cash balances approach as an alternative to Fisher's approach. These economists regarded that, like value theory, the value of money can be determined in terms of supply and demand for money. Robertson argued that, "Money is only one of the many economic things. Its value therefore, is primarily determined by exactly the same two factors as determine the value of any other thing, namely, the conditions of demand for it and the quantity of it available."

According to the cash balance approach the supply of money is exogenously determined, at a point of time by the banking system. Hence, the concept of velocity of money is completely disregarded under this approach. Because, it obscures the motives and decisions of people behind it. The demand for money plays a key role in determining the value of money. Further, it is held that the demand for money is basically the demand to hold cash balances for transactions and precautionary motives.

The cash balance approach concentrates on the demand for money as a store of value and not as a medium of exchange. The Cambridge equations demonstrate that given the supply of money, the value of money is determined by the demand for cash balances. When the demand for money increases, people tend to reduce their expenditures on goods and services and prefer to hold longer amounts of cash. As the demand for goods and services is reduced, it brings down the price level and raise the value of money.

The Cambridge cash balance equations have been developed by Marshall, Pigou, Robertson and Keynes separately which are discussed below :

Marshall's Equation

According to Marshall, the amount an individual wants to hold bears some relation to his income, since that determines the volume of purchases and sales in which he is engaged. These cash balances held by all the individuals in the society, may be added to get the total cash balances as a fraction of their aggregate income. Marshall's Equation is as follows:

$$M = kPY$$

Where,

M stands for exogenously determined supply of money
k is the fraction of the real money income (PY) which people wish to hold in the form of cash
P is the price level
Y is the aggregate real income of the community

As kY remains constant, when M increases P tends to decrease and vice versa. According to Marshall, M and Y being constant, P tends to improve with the increase in k, so k is the more vital factor than M.

Pigou's Equation

Pigou expressed his cash balance approach in the form of equation as follows:

$$P = \frac{kR}{M}$$

Where,

P = the purchasing power of money or the value of money
k = the proportion of total real income (R) which people wish to hold in the form of cash balances
R = total resources or real income expressed in terms of a particular commodity (wheat)
M = the number of actual units of legal tender money.

According to Pigou the demand for money consists of cash or legal money and bank notes and bank balances. To include bank notes and bank balances he modified his equation as:

$$P = \frac{kR}{M} [(c + h (1-c)]$$

Where,

c is the proportion of total real income held by the people in the form of legal tender including token coins.

(1 - C) is the proportion of bank balances held by the people.

h is the proportion of legal tender to deposits held by the banks.

This can be shown diagrammatically as follows:

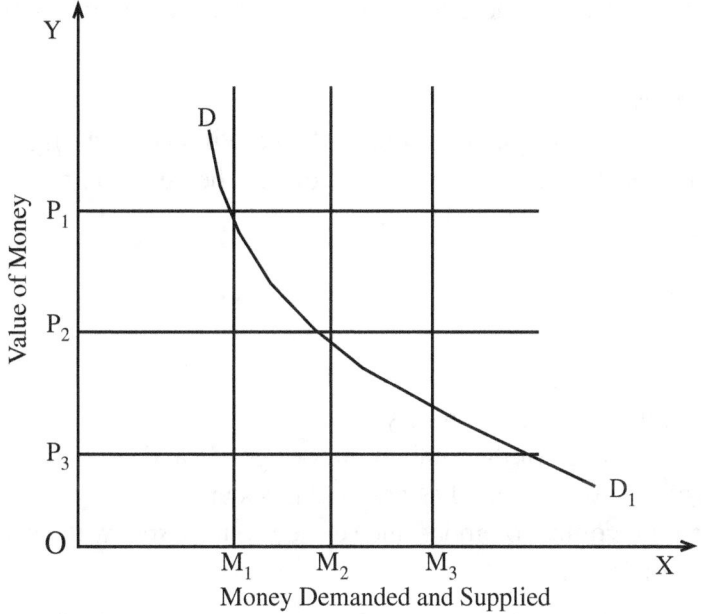

Money Demanded and Supplied

In the figure DD_1 is the demand curve for money and OM_1, OM_2, OM_3 are the supply curves of money based on the assumption that the supply of money at a point of time is fixed.

It is evident from the figure that, when the supply of money increases from OM_1 to OM_2, the value of money is reduced from OP_1 to OP_2 and the decrease in value of money from P_1 to P_2 is exactly equal to the increase in the supply of money by M_1 to M_2. If the supply of money increases by three times from OM_1 to OM_3 the value of money decreases exactly equal from OP_1 to OP_3. The demand curve for money DD_1 is a rectangular hyperbola as it shows changes in the value of money exactly in reverse proportion to the supply of money.

Pigou's equation enables us to conclude that the value of money varies on account of peoples' varying use of money. Sometimes they spend all of their money while at other times they spend only part of the total money and hold rest of the money as money balances.

Keynes has criticised Pigou's equation as follows

i) According to Pigou, R (the real income) in his equation plays an important role because the variation in it has direct impact on k or the demand for money - cash balances but Keynes held that, it is true in case of real deposits only but it is not much significant when the total deposits are taken into consideration.

ii) Pigou has interpreted resources as identical with current income which is not correct.

iii) Pigou has not paid enough attention to the main problem of purchasing power of money in general as he has measured k and R in terms of a single commodity like wheat.

Robertson's Equation

Robertson formulated an equation similar to that of Pigou with the little difference. Robertson included the volume of total transactions in the equation for Pigou's total real resources (R). He stated his equation as:

$$P = \frac{M}{kT}$$

Where,

P = the price level,
M = the total quantity of money,
k = the proportion of the total amount of goods and services (T) which people wish to hold as cash balances and
T = the total volume of goods and services purchased by the people during a period of one year.

This equation implies that the price level P changes directly with M and inversely with k or T.

Keynes' Real Balance Equation

Keynes formulated Real Balance Quantity Equation with a view to improving the other Cambridge equations. He argued that people always keep some purchasing power with them and carry out their day to day transactions. The quantity of purchasing power or the demand for money depends partly on their habits, tastes and preferences and partly on their wealth. The demand for money can be measured in terms of consumption units. A consumption unit is a basket or bundle of standard articles of consumption or other objects of expenditure. The relationship between quantity of money and price level can be explained with the help of following equation:

$$n = pk$$

Where,

n = total currency in circulation
p = price of consumption unit
k = number of consumption units

Thus, a proportionate increase in quantity of money (n) will lead to a proportionate increase in price level (p)

This equation can be extended to include bank deposits. Hence

$$n = p\,(k + rk')$$

Where,

k' = the number of consumption units in the form of bank deposits
r = the cash reserve ratio of banks
As k, k' and r are constant, p will change in the same proportion as the change in n.

Keynes claimed that his equation is superior to other Cambridge equations. The other equations do not indicate how price level can be controlled. Keynes' equation points out that price level p can be regulated by controlling n and r because the cash balances (k) held by the people are outside the control of the monetary authority. Similarly, it is possible to regulate bank deposits k' by suitable changes in the bank rate. Thus, price level can be controlled through appropriate changes in n, r, k' so as to offset changes in k.

Evaluation of Cash Balances Approach

The cash balances approach has been considered as significant improvement over Fisher's transactions approach on account of the following reasons:

i) Cash balances approach was able to overcome the problem of false dichotomy between the theory of value and the theory of money and prices.

ii) In case of cash balances approach money is a stock concept for it refers to cash balances at a point of time while Fisher in his transactions velocity model treated money as a flow concept. This change in approach removed the weakness of transactions approach in providing a satisfactory explanation of the velocity of money.

iii) Cash balances approach concentrates on the demand of money as a strategic explanatory variable while Fisher held that, all fluctuations in general price level could be explained in terms of changes in money supply.

iv) Cash balances approach emphasises store of value as more useful function of money as the people want to hold it. The usefulness of money as a medium of exchange is recognised but it has been given secondary position.

Limitation of Cash balances approach :

i) Narrow View

Equations formulated by Pigou and Keynes suffer from narrow view as they deal with the purchasing power of money in terms of consumption goods only.

ii) Neglect of Key Factors

The cash balances approach gives undue importance to the real income as determinant of k (Cash balance on demand for money). But there are other equally important factors like monetary habits, price level, business combinations etc. which exert strong influence on k which has been completely neglected.

iii) Unrealistic Assumptions

Cash balances approach assumes k and T as given which is not a realistic assumption.

iv) Circular Reasoning

The cash balances approach suffers from circular reasoning. Because it holds that the price level or value of money is determined by the cash holding of the community (k) and at the same time it states that the price level or the value of money determines the amount of cash holdings of the people (k).

v) Neglect of the Role of Rate of Interest

The cash balances approach fails to describe all the forces and processes leading to changes in the price level. It neglects the rate of interest which is closely related to the cash balances and it also affects the production and prices. They treat real income as an independently determined factor.

vi) Role of Real Factors is not recognised

The cash balances approach does not explain the real forces which cause changes in the price level. Several important variables such as saving, investment, income etc. are not taken into consideration. It merely explains that changes in demand for money will result into the changes in the value of money but it does not explain clearly the main factors responsible for bringing about changes in the demand for money.

vii) Unsatisfactory for dealing with Dynamic Conditions

The cash balances approach states that the demand for money has uniform unitary elasticity. But unitary elasticity of demand exists only in static conditions and not under dynamic conditions. The approach fails in providing an adequate monetary explanation of dynamic behaviour in the economy.

viii) Unable to Explain Business Cycles

The cash balances approach fails to provide satisfactory explanation about the occurrence of business cycles especially why prosperity and depression follow one another.

ix) Failure in Explaining Degree of Impact of Changes in Money Supply on Output and Prices

Cash balances approach states that the changes in the quantity of money in short period have an effect in changing output and prices but it fails to explain about the extent of changes in prices and output as a result of a given change in the supply of money.

x) Wrong Conception of the Dichotomy of the Economy

Don Patinkin has pointed out that, the cash balance equation implies that, there is no real balance effect and hence, there is absence of money illusion which is indicated by the homogeneity postulate. The cash balances approach consider a reflection between monetary theory and value theory by assuming dichotomy in the economy i.e. economy is divided in to the real sector and the monetary sector. The real sector is related to the barter economy. The relative values of commodities are expressed in terms of money in the monetary sector. Thus, price level is determined in the monetary sector. In addition to this, the demand function in real sector is assumed to be insensitive to the changes in the price level. This is referring to as homogeneity postulate which indicates the absence of money illusion. If it is regarded that demand function relates to the real sector, then the real values are not affected by the changes in the price level in the monetary sector. Therefore, with changes in the quantity of money there will be equi-proportional changes in the price level.

xi) Neglect of Asset Demand for Money

Cash balances approach considers the choice between consumption and holding money but it overlooks the fact that the choice between holding money as an asset and other financial claims is also important. The cash balances approach has neglected asset demand for money which is functionally related to the rate of interest. The Cambridge economists failed to recognise the possibility of liquidity trap. Now, it is a well known fact that occurrence of the liquidity trap destroys any linkage between money and price.

Conclusion

In spite of these short comings, cash balances approach may be considered as an important contribution towards development of monetary theory. It explains how the changes in decisions of people of holding a part of their real income in cash balances affect the price level. It helps in understanding the problem of value of money. It not only relates the value of money to the changes in the demand for money but also takes into consideration the various motives for holding cash balances of the people.

4.4 MILTON FRIEDMAN'S APPROACH

Milton Friedman in his essay "The Quantity Theory of Money - A Restatement" published in 1956, set down a particular model of quantity theory of money. In his reformulation of the quantity theory, Friedman asserts that the quantity theory is in the first instance a theory of the demand for money. For identifying the key determinants of the demand for money, he classifies the holders of money as between (a) ultimate wealth holders and (b) business enterprises. He emphasizes the role of money as an asset. He generalizes Keynes' analysis of the speculative demand for money by treating the total demand for money as a part of wealth theory concerned with the composition of the portfolios of assets. Because of its peculiar property as the generally acceptable means of payments, money is assumed to yield a flow of services to its holder.

Each of the following assets has distinctive attributes and each yield some return in terms of money or in kind.

Money yields return generally in kind, in the form of convenience, security etc. Sometimes money yields return in the form of money. For example, saving deposits with banks earn interest. However, the real yield of money depends on the changes in the price level. When the general price level falls, the value of money increases, so that there is a capital gain in real terms which should be added to the nominal yield. On the other hand, when the general price level rises inflationary conditions tend to dominate and the value of money falls and hence, there is a capital loss in real terms, which should be deducted from the nominal yield.

Bonds are another type of asset in which the people can hold their wealth. Bonds are securities which yield a flow of income in the form of interest, fixed in nominal terms. Yield on bond is the coupon rate of interest. The real income from the bonds is affected by changes in the price level and rate of interest on the bonds.

Equities or shares are a form of asset in which wealth can be held. These are the assets which promise a perpetual income stream of constant real amount. The yield from equity is determined by the dividend rate, expected capital gains or loss and expected changes in the price level.

The fourth form in which people hold their wealth is physical goods like stock of producer or capital goods and consumer durable goods. These goods yield a stream of income in kind, which cannot be measured explicitly in terms of rate of interest. However, their nominal rate of return is affected by the rate of change in the price level.

According to Friedman, total wealth is composed of both human and non-human wealth. Human wealth is difficult to measure because the conversion of human into non-human wealth or non-human into human wealth is subject to institutional constraints. These restrictions cannot be measured in terms of market prices or rates of return. However, there is a possibility of substituting human wealth to non-human wealth and vice versa. Friedman calls the ratios of non-human to human wealth or ratio of wealth to income as W and argues that the level of permanent income (X) and wealth (W) point toward the income elasticity of demand for money which is greater than unity.

Friedman's nominal demand function (Md) for money is as :

$$Md = f(w, h, rm, rb, re, p, \frac{\Delta p}{p}, u)$$

The demand for real money balances is nominal demand for money divided by the price level. So the demand for real money balances can be written as –

Where Md stands for nominal demand for money.

stands for demand for real money balances

w stands for wealth of individuals

h for the proportion of human wealth to the total wealth held by the individuals

rm for rate of return or interest on money

rb for rate of interest on bonds

re for rate of return on equities

p for price level

$\dfrac{\Delta p}{p}$ for change in price level or rate of inflation

u for institutional factors.

Simplifying Friedman's Demand for Money Function –

The main problem in using Friedman's demand for money function is that of non-availability of reliable data about the value of wealth (w) hence, in practice it is difficult to estimate demand for money. To overcome this difficulty Friedman has suggested that, since the present value of wealth or

$W = \dfrac{Yp}{r}$ (where Yp is the permanent income and r is the rate of interest on money), permanent income Yp may be used as the variable for wealth. When these changes are made, we get Friedman's demand for money function in simplified form as

$$Md = (Yp, h, rm, rb, re, \frac{\Delta P}{P}, u)$$

If we assume that no price change is anticipated and institutional factors such as h and u remain constant in the short run and all the three rates of interests grouped together into one interest rate, then we get Friedman's demand for money function in simple form as :

$$Md = f(Yp, r)$$

When we compare this demand function with the Keynesian demand function, we find that, they are more or less similar. But there are three main differences –

i) There is emphasis on current income in Keynesian approach while Friedman's approach emphasizes wealth.

ii) In Friedman's approach no unstable element is involved as it is implied by the speculative demand for money in Keynesian approach.

iii) In Friedman's approach there is nothing to suggest that elasticity of demand for money with respect to the rate of interest will become infinite at some positive rate of interest. In other words it does not expect any possibility of a liquidity trap.

Comparison of the Transactions Approach and the Cash Balances Approach

There are certain points of similarities between Quantity Theory and Cash Balances Theory

1. Same Conclusion : Both Quantity Theory and Cash Balances theory lead to the same conclusion that there is a direct and proportional relationship between the quantity of money and the price level and an inverse proportionate relationship between the quantity of money and the value of money.

2. Similarity in Equations : Robertson's cash balances equation and Fisher's cash transactions equation are more or less similar in form. Although, there is apparent difference in V and k, but k and V are reciprocals of each other.

3. Money as the Same Phenomenon : The different symbols given to the total quantity of money in the two approaches refer to same phenomenon. As such MV+M'V' of Fisher's equation, M of the equation of Pigou and Robertson, and n of Keynes' equation refer to the total quantity of money.

In spite of certain similarities, there are significant differences between these two approaches.

4.5   DIFFERENCE BETWEEN QUANTITY THEORY AND CASH BALANCE THEORY

1. Functions of Money : Fisher's approach considers the medium of exchange function of money whereas Cambridge approach emphasises the store of value function of money.

2. Flow and Stock : The transactions approach is based on a flow concept of money whereas the cash balances approach is based upon stock concept of money.

3. V and k Different : The transactions approach emphasises the spending approach of money so V is very significant. But cash balances approach stresses the holding aspect of money hence k becomes important element.

4. Nature of Price Level : In Quantity Theory of Money P refers to the average price level of all goods and services. But in the Cash Balances Theory P refers to the prices of final or consumer goods.

5. Nature of T : In Quantity Theory of Money T refers to the total amount of goods and services exchanged for money. But in the Cash Balances Theory T refers to the final or consumer goods exchanged for money.

6. Emphasis on Supply and Demand for Money : The Quantity Theory of Money emphasises the supply of money, whereas the cash balances theory emphasises both the demand for money and the supply of money.

7. Different in Nature : The two theories are different in nature. The Quantity Theory of Money is mechanistic because it does not explain how changes in V bring about changes in P. On the other hand, the Cash Balances Theory is realistic because it studies the psychological factors which influence k.

QUESTIONS

1. Explain the Quantity Theory of Money.
2. Explain the Cambridge Cash Balance Approach.
3. Comment on Milton Friedman's Approach.
4. What is the difference between Quantity Theory and Cash Balance Theory?

Chapter 5	INFLATION AND DEFLATION

CONTENTS

INTRODUCTION

Inflation is a macroeconomic phenomenon. The rise in the general price level or fall in the value of money is the main feature of inflation. In simple and common man's language inflation means price rise. When prices of all goods and services are rising on an average continuously over the period of time then economy is facing inflation. Inflation decreases the value of money. It has effect on different sector of the economy like producers, investors, fixed wage earners etc. The effects of inflation depend upon the rate of inflation. If inflation is moderate it is said to be beneficial for the economy. But a very high rate of inflation causes many economic and social problems.

5.1 INFLATION AND DEFLATION- MEANING, CAUSES AND EFFECTS

Inflation is defined as a rise in general price level. It is a commonly used word and has been one of the important problems facing major economies in the world. Different economists have given definition of inflation which is as below:

Brooman defines inflation as "Inflation is a continuing rise in general price level."

Crowther defines inflation as "a state in which the value of money is falling i.e. prices are rising."

According to Friedman "Inflation is always and everywhere a monetary phenomenon, and it can be produced only by a more rapid increase in the quantity of money than output." But the other economists argue that money supply alone is not the cause of inflation.

Prof. Coulbourn defines inflation as a situation where there is "too much money chasing too few goods."

Prof. Samuelson simply defines inflation as "Inflation occurs when the general level of prices and cost is rising."

J.M. Keynes defined inflation as "an expansion in the supply of money relatively to the supply of things to purchase." Keynes argued that, so far as there is underemployment in the economy, an increase in money supply leads to increase in aggregate demand, output and employment. Any rise in price level before full employment is reached called as "bottleneck inflation" or "semi inflation." When money supply increases beyond the full employment level, then output does not increase, and prices rise in proportion to with the rise in money supply. This is called as "true inflation" by Keynes. Thus for Keynes "inflation is a post full employment phenomenon.

From the above definitions of inflation, it is true that rising prices are an important symptom of inflation. But every increase in prices does not mean that there is inflation. It is said to exist when the price level rises persistently and rapidly.

Nature or Characteristics of Inflation

i) Inflations is a process of continuously rising general price level.
ii) Inflation is a long term and dynamic process.
iii) Inflation is a sustained and appreciable rise in prices.
iv) It is a phenomenon which comes into existence only after full employment.
v) It is a monetary phenomenon.
vi) It is characterized by excess demand where too much money chases too few goods.
vii) It is characterized by rise in money income.
viii) It is anticipated, that one can not be sure regarding the timing and intensity of inflation.
ix) It leads to further rise in prices.
x) It is irreversible in nature.
xi) It is a full in external value of money as measured by foreign exchange rates or by price of gold.
xii) The rate of inflation is the rate of change of the general price level.

Types of Inflation

Inflation occurs in the economy due to increase in the money incomes of some sections of population without equivalent increase in production or output. It gives rise to an increase in the aggregate demand for goods and services which cannot be met at current prices by the total available supply of goods and services in the country. So the prices of goods and services start rising.

(1) Inflation can be classified into following types, on the basis of rate of Inflation.

(i) Creeping Inflation :

It is the mildest form of inflation and is not considered to have dangerous effects on the economy. Creeping inflation is through to be inevitable consequence of economic growth. It provides incentive for investment as it helps to earn profit for inefficient firms. It does not allow economy to stagnate.

According to others, even creeping inflation is harmful to the economy as they consider inflation similar to conception. It looks simple and harmless in the beginning but with passage of time it may assume dangerous proportions. Hence it must be nipped in the bud. According to Kent, when prices rise by not more than 3 percent per annum, the situation may be described as that of creeping inflation.

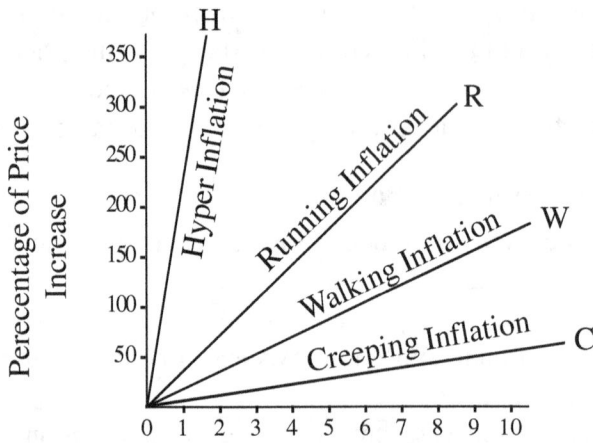

Figure : Time (years)

(ii) Walking Inflation :

It is considered as mild and tolerable form of inflation. When the rate of inflation is less than 10 percent per annum, it is called as walking or trotting inflation. It refers to the 3 to a percent price rise per annum. During this type of inflation expectations of the people tend to remain stable, hence it is described stable inflation. It is single digit inflation.

(iii) Running Inflation :

When the prices rise continuously at a rate more than 10 percent per annum, running inflation comes, into existence, According to Samuelson when the prices are rising at a rate of double or triple digit i.e. 20%, 200% per annum then the situation is described as galloping inflation. This type of inflation is very serious problem, which causes sever distortions and disturbances in the economy. Many countries in the world, including India have either walking inflation or running infation.

Hyper Inflation

When prices rise every moment and there is no limit to the highest rate of price rise then it is called hyper inflation. It's magnitude is difficult to measure because prices rise suddenly at any moment. When prices rise at a rate of 1000 percent per annum, the purchasing power of the people reaches at a very low level, real wages decrease rapidly and inequalities tend to increase significantly. It may lead to serious disruptions and distortions in the economy and may lead to social revolution. Germany suffered from hyper inflation in 1920-1923.

Causes of Inflation

The main factors responsible for inflation is generally excess demand. The factors that cause excess demand are the factors which result in inflation. Excess demand may be the result of upward shift in demand or downward shift in supply. Let us discuss these factors briefly.

A) Factors Affecting Demand

Monetarists and Keynesians belives that inflation is mainly due to factors which cause an upward shift in the aggregate demand. The main factors causing this shift are as discussed below :

1) Increase in money supply

The main cause of excess monetary demand is increase in money supply, which leads to increase in disposable income or purchasing power with the people. It tends to increase demand for goods and services in the economy.

2) Increase in government expenditure

Rapid increase in huge government expenditure on development projects with longer gestation period generates money income immediately in the hands of the public, but there is no corresponding increase in output hence price level starts rising and inflationary pressures generate in the economy.

3) Deficit financing

Developing countries adopt deficit financing policy to promote economic development of the country. It only results in rapid increase in money income and purchasing power of the people. It raises aggregate demand in relation to aggregate supply and cause inflationary rise in prices it is known as deficit induced inflation.

4) Excessive creidt creation by commerical banks

When commerical banks create excessive credit and it is used for unproductive purposes and speculative activities, then it contributes to rise in price level.

5) Rapid Expansion of Private sector

The expansion of private sector through huge investments increase employment and income in the economy. It results in creating demand for goods and services. But it takes time for output to enter the market. Hence general price rise become common.

6) Black Money

Several malpractices such as corruption, tax evasion etc generates black money on which government has no control. Hence such money is spent extravagently which creates unnecessary demand for goods and services. This may lead to rise in the price level.

7) Repayment of Public Debt

Whenever the government repays its past debt to the public, it increases money supply and purchasing power with the public. This may lead to increase in the aggregate demand for goods and services and general price rise in the economy.

8) Increase in Exports

When demand for domestically produced goods increase in foreign countries, this increase earnings of exporters which may create more demand for goods and services in the economy.

9) Higher Growth of Population

Higher rate of growth of population stimulates effective demand to rise while aggregate supply cannot be increased correspondingly. Hence price rise becomes inevitable in a over populated economy.

B) Factors Affecting Supply

There are certain factors which affect supply side and it results in downward shift in supply. These factors may be stated as follows :

1) Shortage of factors of production

Shortage of factors of productions such as capital skilled labour, raw materials etc which results in excess capacity and reductions in industral production. Hence aggreagate supply falls short of demand for it.

2) Instability of agricultural production

Agricultural production is subject to seasonal variations as it is dependent on natural factors. Shortages of food gains and raw materials for agrobased industries may give rise to inflationary conditions in the economy.

3) Arficial Scarcities

The hoarders and speculators interntionally create scarcities of essential commodities which tends to develop black marketing activities on a wider scale. This may result in reducing supplies of goods and raising their prices.

4) Increase in Exports

When the demand for exports increases rapidly then domestic availability of goods tends to decrease in local markets. This may result in inflation in the economy.

5) Law of Diminishing Returns

As the most of the industries use old machine and outdated methods of production, the diminishing returns start seprating soon. This not only reduces level of production but also increase cost of productions, which may result in rise in prices of the products produced.

6) Lop sided production

With a view to earn more profit, producers may concentrate on production of luxury goods and the production of mass consumption goods tends to be neglected. On account of shortage of consumer goods, their prices rise rapidly giving rise to inflation in the economy.

7) Lack of Entrepreneurship

Lack of entrepreneurship tends to reduce productive activities in the economy and hence aggregate supply cannot increase at a faster rate.

8) Industrial Disputes

When trade unions are well organised and strong they insist on higher wages without corresponding increase in the productivity of the workers and often go on strike. Sometimes industrialist find it difficult to satisfy their demands and they declare lock outs. As a result production falls and supply of goods is reduced. As a result price rise may take place.

9) International factors

When prices rise in developed countries, their effects are spread over other countries through foreign trade. Rise in price of important input like crude oil and Petrol in the international market may result in rise in prices of several other commodities.

10) Shortage of Foreign Exchange

Developing countries have to face the problem of adverse balance of payments due to shortages of foreign exchange earnings. These economics are in need of foreign exchange for importing technology and scarce raw materials. This shortages of foreign exchange tend to hamper industrial growth in developing economies.Hence total supply position in the economy cannot be improved significantly.

11) Non-economic factors

Wars, inefficiency, poor law and order situation, corruption, lack of sence of responsible citizenship etc provide fertile breed in ground for inflation.

Consequences of Inflation or Effects of Inflation

According to some economists mild inflation is desirable as it provides incentive for investment and stimulates production. But others are worried about socio economic consequences of inflation and hence they describe it as enemy number one.

Inflation affects different people differently because of the fall in the value of money. When prices rise, some group of people in a society gain while others lose. Mild inflation may help in achieving full employment but unless it is controlled it gives rise to evils and affects economic, social, political and moral life of the people. The main effects or consequences of inflation are discussed below.

(A) Effects on production

It is generally belived that a mild inflation stimulates production when there are unemployed resources, because it creates optimistic expectations about profit margins. But if inflation gets momentum and reaches an advanced stage it adversely affects production. The effects of inflation on production may be discussed as follows.

i) Misallocation of Resources

Under inflation, producers divert resources from production of mass consumption goods to luxury goods and consumer durable products in order to earn more profits.

ii) Encouragement to speculation

Inflation promotes activition of businessmen mainly for speculation for earning quick profit. Hence production suffers as speculation takes place of production.

iii) Hoarding and Black marketing

During inflation holding stocks of essential goods becomes more profitable. So hoarding is encouraged. This reduces supply of available goods and thus encourages black marketing. Thus, profit seekers easily earn hype profits by mainpulating markets.

iv) Avoiding Risks of Production

Under the stage of inflation, the entrepreneurs are discouraged from taking risks which are involved in production for the future.

v) Sellers' Market

Under inflationary conditious, whatever is produced is quickly sold in the markets. This generates sellers' inflation. Since producesr and sellers all aim at earning quick profits, it advergely affects the quality of products.

vi) Reduction in Production Volume

Inflation adversely affects the volume of production because the expectation of rising prices alongwith rising costs of inputs give rise to atmosphere of uncertainty. Hence production volume is likely to be contracted.

vii) Reduction in inflow of foreign capital

Inflation discourages inflow of foreign capital because rising costs of materials and other inputs tend to make foreign investment less profitable.

viii) Adverse effect on Investment and capital formation.

When prices rise rapidly, savings tend to decrease because most of the income of the people is spent on consumption due to high prices, which reduces investment and capital formation in the economy.

(B) Effects on Distribution of Income and wealth

The impact of inflation is felt unevenly by various groups in the society. It is believed that inflation hits hard to fixed income groups than to high and flexible income group people. Let us study effects of inflation on various groups in the society.

i) Debtors and creditors

During inflation the debtors as group tend to gain as they repay debts in future, they would pay back less value as the value of money depreciates than what they had borrowed. Creditors to that extent tend to be the losers as they get less value when the debts are paid back is future. Rate of interest charged for debt tends to be lower than the rate of growth of inflation.

ii) Business community

Enterpreneurs and businessman prefer inflation because their profit margins tend to increase with prices rising more than the cost of production. During inflation value of inventories appreciates although the cost of production remains constant.

iii) Fixed Income Groups and Salaries People

Under inflation low income group people and fixed income earners are hit very hard. During inflation wages and salaries do not increase in the same proportion as price rise. Hence such people have to suffer heavily during inflationary conditions in the economy.

iv) Investors

The effect of inflation on investors depend upon whether they invest in fixed interest earning securities or equities. If they invest in fixed income earning securities then they tend to lose, but if they invest in equities they tend to gain. Because prices of securities do not increase with inflation but equity prices generally increase along with inflation mostly at the same rate. As Keynes has stated. "Inflation has not only diminished the capacity of investing class to save, but has destroyed the atmosphere of confidence which is a condition of willingness to save."

v) Agriculturists

During inflation the prices of foodgrains rise faster than the cost of production, hence the farmers gain. But landless agricultural labourers are hit hard, as their wages do not increase by the farmers.

vi) Government

The Government as a debtor gains at the expense of households which are mostly the creditors. The interest rates in government bonds are fixed and do not change with the rise in prices. During inflation redistribution of wealth takes place in favour of government.

Thus, inflation results in redistribution of income and wealth in the society. Wages and salary earness and fixed income groups lose while profit earners gain. The creditors lose while debtors gain.

(C) Other Consequences

The other effects of inflation may be discussed as under.

1) Government

Inflation affects government in various ways. Government uses inflationary finance for financing its various activities. It leads to the increase in money income of the people, part of which is collected by the government by way of taxes on incomes and commodities. As a result government revenues tend to increase during inflation. Under rising prices the real burden of money debt tends to decrease. The government expenditure tends to increase on account of increase in production costs of developmental projects and public enterprises and expenditure on administration also increase on account of wages and salary increase. Hence inflation increases revenue of government but the government expences also increases with rising production cost of public projects, increase in administrative expences and wage rise.

2) Balance of Payments

When prices rise rapidly in a home country as compared to other countries, then domestic products become costly hence exports are reduced while imports are encouraged. Thus, adverse balance of payments situation arises.

When prices rise at a higher rate in the home country than in other countries then it becomes necessary to reduce the exchange rate in relation to foreign countries.

Inflation affects adversely the balance of payment of a country. When prices rise more rapidly in the home country than in foreign countries then domestic products become costly compared to foreign products. This tends to increase imports and reduce exports, thereby making the balance of payments unfavoarable.

3) Collapse of Monetary System

Under the conditions of prolonged hyperinflation value of money depreciates rapidly and ultimately it leads to the collapse of monetary system. It happened in Gemany after the world war I.

4) Social Consequences

Inflation is socially harmful. It widens the gap between the rich and poor. Inflation increase dissatisfaction among the masses. Workers demand more wages and when their demands are not accepted by the management they go on strike. Hence productions in the economy decreases. In order to make quick profits, people adopt practices like hording, black marketing, speculation etc and corruption develops rapidly in the society. All these developments tend to reduce efficiency of the economy significantly.

Political Consequences

Rising prices give rise to agitations and protests by opposition parties and start criticing government policies and try to bring pressure on government to take steps to control inflation at any cost. Many governments have lost their power on account of inflation.

Conclusion

Inflation is socially undersirable. It results in increase of hard-ships to the masses. It discoureges production, results in artillary distribution of income and wealth. It breaks down public morals, pollutes moral and ethical life of people, and prepares the ground for social and political up heavals.

Deflation

As inflation is associated with the rise in the price level, deflation is a phenomenon associated with a steady and sustained fall in the level of prices. In other words deflation is just opposite of Inflation. Although deflation is characterised by falling prices every fall in prices cannot be called as deflation. For example, fall in prices after inflation has reached its peak cannot be described as deflation. Such a fall is disinflationary and not deflationary, because it does not result in any unemployment, and reduction in output in the economy. Thus, only that fall in prices which results in unemployment and reduction in output is deflationary in nature. In other words, deflation is that state where every fall in prices causes unemployment and fall in incomes of the factors of production in the economy.

Definitions

i) According to Coulborn, deflation is a state in which the value of money is rising or prices are falling. It is associated with falling activity and unemployment. Involuntary unemployment is the hall mark of deflation.

ii) Paul Einzing defines deflation as a state of disequilibrium in which contraction of economic power tends to cause or is the effect of a decline of price level." Deflation refers to a situation where prices fall causing substantial increase in unemployment, reduction in output and decrease in incomes.

iii) Misra and Puri define deflation as "a process in which persistent and appreciable fall in the general price level is acompanied by a considerable amount of involuntary unemployment."

Causes of Deflation

A) Factors affecting Demand

  i) Decrease in money supply
 ii) Decrease in Government expenditure
iii) Surplus budgeting
 iv) Scarcity of credit facilities
  v) Slow growth of private sector
 vi) Raising of public debt
vii) Decrease in exports
viii) Low growth or stagnant of population etc.

B) Factors affecting supply side

 1) Abundant supply of factors of production
 2) Agricultural prosperity
 3) Increase in imports
 4) Technological progress leading to gluts in markets.
 5) Rapid growth of enterprires
 6) Industrial peace
 7) Stable government with liberal policies
 8) Peace and order in the economy
 9) Favourable international environment
10) Surplus balance of payment and foreign exchanges reserves etc.

Consequences of deflation or effects of deflation

The consequences or effects of deflation are opposite to those of inflation. Deflation affects different groups of people differently. These effects are discussed below.

A) Effects on Production

As deflation is characterised by continuous fall in the general price level, it adversely effects production as well as employment. During deflation the whole economy is dominated by pessimism. Investors are not willing to make investments and hence the national income decline significantly. Deflation results in increase in idle capacity in various sectors of the economy. Marginal efficiency of capital reaches minimum level and even investments of replacement of depreciated plant and equipment is postponed. In extreme cases investment may tend to be nagative.

During deflation the aggregate expenditure in the economy is much less than the value of current output, which is described as deflationary gap. On account of continuous falling prices produces curtail production and employment. During deflation markets are glutted with goods but matching response from customers is absent. Thus a situation of "poverty amongst plenty" is created.

B) Effects on Distribution

During deflation redistribution of income and wealth may take place but no one is significantly benefited. Deflation tends to distribute income in favour of middle class or rentier class but adversely affects the interests of businessmen, debtors and farmers. Since most cost are sticky downward, when prices fall profits are reduced substantially. On account of continuous fall of effective demand involuntary accumulation of stocks starts rising involving unnecessary storage costs. As the demand for non food crops decrease, farmers shift to food grain crops which leads to further fall in the price level. During deflation, bargaining position of workers tend to be very weak and they have to accept wage cuts. As a result along with money wages real wages also decline. Rentiers are benefited as rent are not revised downward. They experience stability in their incomes, who enjoy benefits while rest of the people continue to suffer. Cerditors may be benefited as the amount of interest receive by them is more in terms of purchasing power. The real worth of principal also increase as compared to the past, when the loan was given. However a large number of loans sanctioned before the period of deflation tend to be lost as bad debts. Regular debtors paying interest changes regularly and repay loans continue to be sufferers.

Comparison between Inflation and deflation

Inflation and deflation both are equally bad in their effects on society. But inflation is the lesser evil. As Keynes has stated, "Inflation is unjust, deflation is inexpedient, of the two deflation is worse"

Inflation leads to rising prices and redistributions of income in favure of better off classes where as deflation leads to fall in output, employment income in favour of better off classes whereas deflation leads to fall in output, employment and income in a capitalist society out of many evils, unemployment leading to poverty is the worst.

Inflation is worst because it widens the gap between the rich and poor. It make rich more rich and the poor are made poorer.

Inflation is unjust because persons who save are losers in the long run. Deflation is inexpedient or inadvisiable on moral grounds because it reduces national income, output and employment. Inflation take away half the bread of the poor, deflation takes away the whole of it, because there is mass unemployment during falling prices.

Depression is inexpedient because it leads to depression making all economic activities stagnant. Even goods crops bring poverty to the farmars.

Although inflation and deflation both are evils and hence be avoided, still we preferred inflation because it increases national output employment and income, secondly, it is also easier to control inflation than deflation through monetary fiscal and direct control measures. Thirdly inflation leads to increase inequalities of income and wealth on social services by government. Thus, the government is better equipped to handle ill effects of inflation than those of deflation. Finally, so long as inflation is mild it stimulates the economy to grow. It is only when inflation becomes hyper inflation it become dangerous. Still its effects on the economy are not so injurious as those of deflation. Thus, out of the two unavoidable inflation may be preferred than deflation.

5.2 DEMAND PULL AND COST PUSH INFLATION

Demand pull inflation or excess demand inflation is the traditional and most common type of inflation. It takes place when aggregate demand is rising while the available supply of goods is becoming less.

An excess of aggregate demand over available supply causes prices to rise. Inflation resulting in this manner is described as demand pull inflation because prices are pulled upwards by excessive total demand.

According to Keynes demand is the important cause of inflation. An excess of aggregate demand over available supply causes prices to rise is described as demand pull inflation. The concept of demand pull inflation is generally associated with a situation of full employment. When the resources are not fully employed an increase in demand will generally force the producer to use the unutilized resources and increase the supply. Under such a situation prices are not likely to increase. But once the resources are fully employed the aggregate supply can not increase in response to increase in demand. This results in rise in prices due to excess demand. The concept of demand pull inflation can be explained with the help of following diagram:

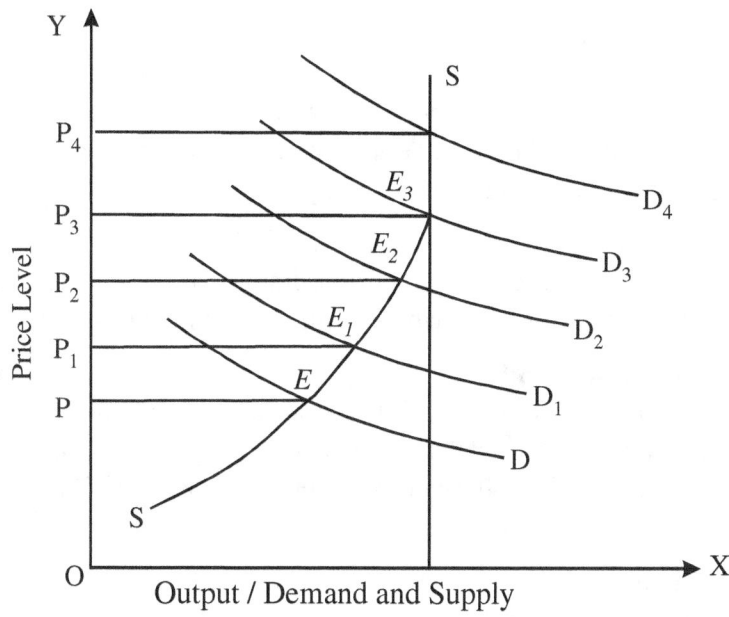

The phenomenon of demand pull inflation has been explained in the above diagram. The X axis measures demand and supply and Y axis measures price levels. The curve D, D1, D2, D3 and D4 shows the rising aggregate demand. S is the aggregated supply curve. As it is full employment level, it is not possible for the economy to increase in supply. D curve is the initial demand curve which intersects the supply curve at point E and therefore OP is the price level. When demand increases the demand curve shifted to the right as D1, D2 and so on, as the economy has not yet reached the full employment level, the price level rises slowly from OP1 to OP2 to OP3. At the point E3, the stage of full employment is reached. Any further increase in demand will result in a sharp increase in price level i.e. OP3 to OP4. According to Keynes the rise in price level from OP3 to OP4 is the 'true inflation' and it is known as demand pull inflation.

Causes of Demand-pull Inflation

Demand pull inflation arises only when, there is a full employment and hence any increase in aggregate demand cannot be matched corresponding increase in the supply of goods and services. There are many causes giving rise to the excess monetary demand there are as follows.

i) Increase in government expenditure

In order to finance for economic development goverment adopts deficit budget policy, which results in siginficant increase in demand which cannot be met by increasing production of goods and services. so excess monetary demand arises which leads to demand pull inflation.

ii) Increase in Investment

Firms may increase autonomous investment which is in excess of current savings in the economy. There is increase in expenditure and aggregate damand but real output may not increase as required hence excess monetary demand may result in overall increase in the general price level in the economy.

iii) Increase in Marginal propensity to consume (MPC)

Sometimes increase in the MPC under the impact of demonstration effect etc. may lead to excess monetary demand which results in demand push inflation.

iv) Surplus Balance of payments

Increase in exports over imports leads to the surplus balance of payments situation which tends to generate higher money incomes as export earnings in the economy. But as goods are exported there is a shortage of domestic goods which leads to demand pull inflation.

v) Diverfication of resources

When the resources are diverted from consumptions goods sector to capital goods sector or the defence sector that also leads to demand pull inflation because of increase in expenditure is not correspondingly met with increase in production of goods demanded by consumers.

Cost Push Inflation:

The rise in price level due to increase in cost of production is called as cost push inflation. According to this theory, there is a rise in the cost of production which pushes up the level of prices leading to cost push inflation. Total cost of production consist of wages, rent, interest, cost on raw material, electricity charges, taxes, advertisement cost, transport cost etc. when any of these cost increases which result in pushing up the level of prices and generating cost push inflation. Increase in wages to be a major factor leading to inflation and therefore the cost push inflation is also referred to as wage push inflation.

The concept of cost push inflation can be presented diagrammatically as follows:

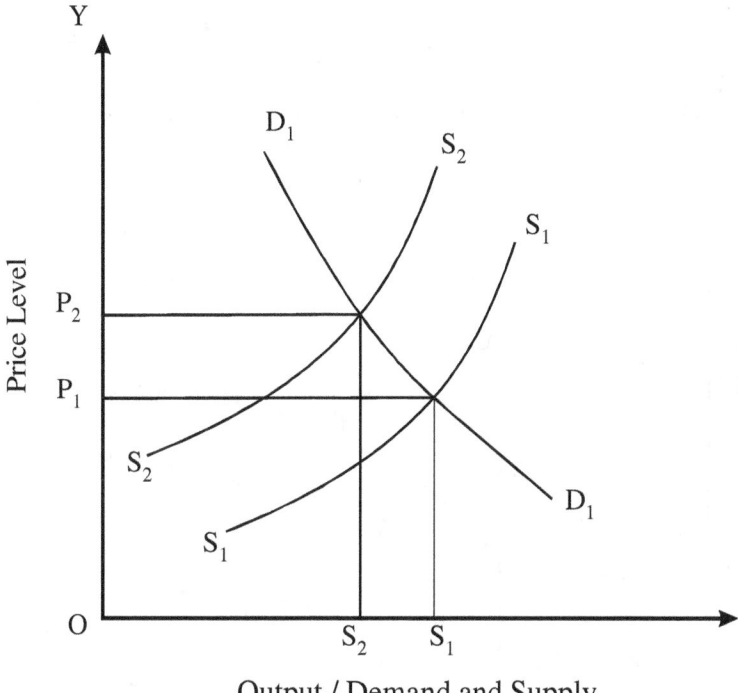

Output / Demand and Supply

The demand for and supply of goods and services represented on the X axis. OS1 is the output demanded and supplied at the price OP1. Now the shift in the supply curve due to increase in costs to the left be represented by S2S2 pushing price up form OP1 to OP2. In this way rise in costs result rise in prices is called as cost push inflation.

Causes of Cost-push inflation :
  (1) Increase in labour cost or wages and income increase price level.
  (ii) Cost push inflation can also be generated by rise in raw material costs.
  (iii) If the indirect taxes are increased cost of production also increase.
  (iv) In developing countries lack of efficient infrastructure facilities like electricity transports, communication etc. leads to high cost of production and to price rise.

5.3 INFLATIONARY GAP

The concept of inflationary gap was stated by Keynes. Keynes in his essay "How to pay for the war" in 1940 described inflation in terms of Inflationary gap. Keynes stated that excess expenditure over full employment income is the main determinant of inflation. According to Keynes inflationary gap exist when beyond full employment level aggregate demand exceeds aggregate supply.

According to Lipsey "The inflationary gap is the amount by which aggregate expenditure exceeds aggregate output at full employment level of income."

Prof. Kurihara define inflationary gap "as an excess of anticipated expenditure over available output."

In short inflationary gap is the gap between aggregate demand and aggregate real output which is presented diagrammatically as follow:

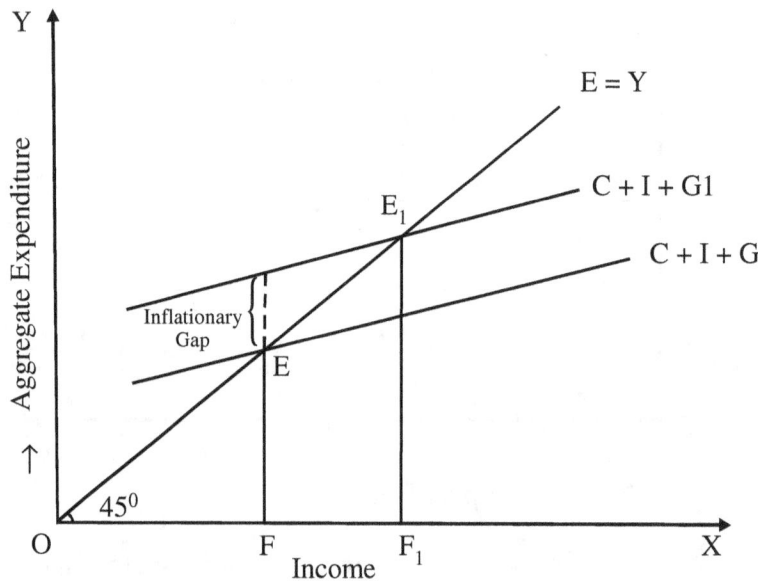

In the above diagrammed Y axis represent aggregate expenditure by household (C) Firm (I) and Government (G). X axis show real income or output of goods and services. E = Y is the 45«% line show the equality between expenditure and real income.

C+I+G curve represent total expenditure including consumption, investment and government expenditure. Initial equilibrium of the economy is at point E which represent full employment at OF. Beyond OF the output cannot be increased. But when government expenditure increases aggregate expenditure curve shift from C+I+G to C+I+G1. The new equilibrium will be at point E1. This means the aggregate demand has increased.

Real output remain OF while aggregate demand shift to E1 from E. This is the situation of excess demand creating inflationary gap. The distance E-E1 is the inflationary gap according to Keynes.

There exist positive functional relationship between inflationary gap and rate of inflation. The larger the gap, the faster will be rise in price level.

Inflationary gap guide how to implement appropriate monetary and fiscal measures to control inflation. Government can take necessary action to control the aggregate demand or to increase real output. Inflationary gap analysis clearly gives excess demand as the source of inflation.

5.4 PHILLIPS CURVE- SUPPLY SIDE ECONOMICS

An empirical study of inflation was undertaken by the noted British economist A.W. Phillips. On the basis of data of the U.K. for the period from 1861 to 1957, Phillips found a relationship between money wages and unemployment rate. Phillips came to the conclusion that there is an inverse relationship between the rate of inflation and the rate of unemployment. Phillips studied the relationship between a number of macro variables like prices, wages and unemployment.

The Phillips curve is a graphic representation of the relationship between inflation and unemployment. The short run Phillips curve is presented as follows:-

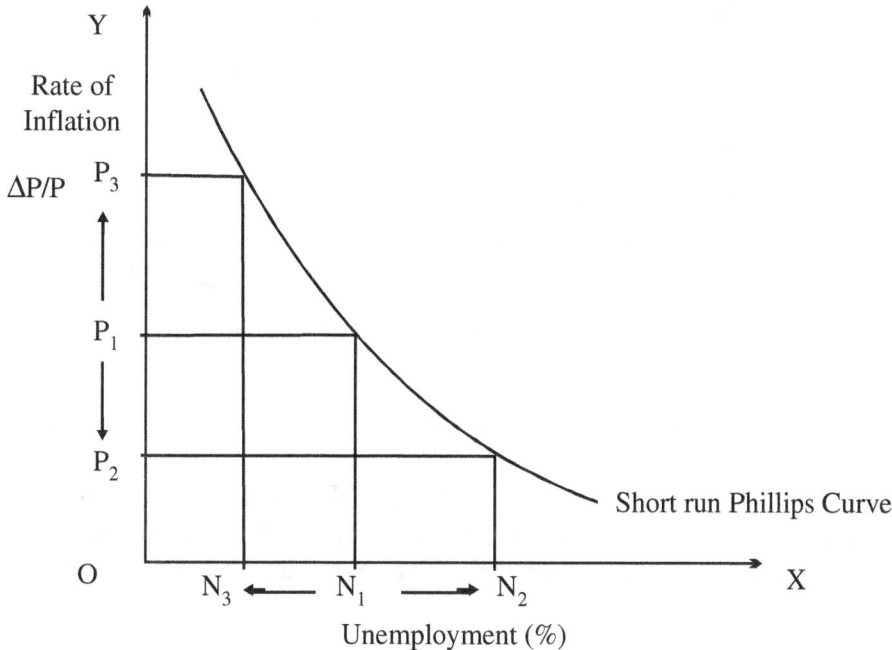

The short run Phillips Curve explains the trade-off between inflation and unemployment. It implies that every country has to choose between two major economic problems of inflation and unemployment. If a country attempts to achieve the objective of having a low rate of unemployment, it will face the problem of experiencing a high rate of inflation.

On the other hand, if it controls the problem of inflation, it would suffer from a high level of unemployment in the economy. Since it is a choice between two major economic problems facing an economy, it is called a trade-off; one problem can be resolved only at the cost of another.

The Phillips curve became a vertical line, parallel to the Y axis in the long run which is presented as follows:

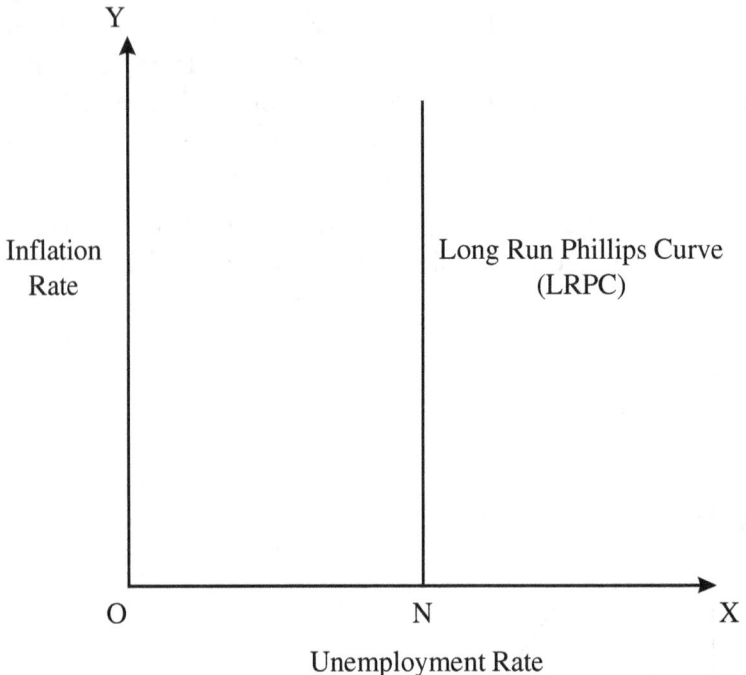

In the above diagram the Long Run Phillips Curve (LRPC) is represented as a vertical straight line parallel to the Y axis. As is seen in the diagram above the LRPC is vertical at point N. Point N is the Non-accelerating Inflation Rate of Unemployment (NAIRU). It is a natural rate of unemployment. The NAIRU is the lowest unemployment rate that can be sustained without upward pressure on inflation.

Criticism of Phillips Curve:
1) Phillips analysis ignores the role of trade unions in the labour market which can shift the curve.
2) The Phillips curve analysis assumes inflation as the internal problem of a country and relates it with the domestic labour market. It ignores the fact that inflation in modern times is an international phenomenon and domestic variables do not have much influence on it.
3) There exists a two-way relationship between wages and prices. Both influence each other and are influenced by each other.
4) The problem of stagflation can not be explained by this analysis.

5.5 STAGFLATION

Stagflation is a new term which has been added to economic literature in the 1970s. The word "Stagflation" is the combination of stag plus flation, taking 'stag' from stagnation and 'flation' from inflation. Thus it is a paradoxical situation where the economy experiences stagnation or unemployment alonwith a high rate of inflation. Therefore, it is also called inflationary recession.

Stagflation refers to a simultaneous growth of inflation and unemployment. The co-existence of unemployment and inflation is called as stagflation. One of the principal causes of stagflation has been restriction in the aggregate supply. When aggregate supply is reduced, there is a fall in output and employment and the price level rises.

During 1960's Phillips curve remained popular among the economist and policy makers. According to Prof. A.W. Phillips, there is an inverse relationship between unemployment and inflation. But from 1967 onward the industrially developed countries of the world are experiencing simultaneous growth of inflation and unemployment. This new phenomenon of co-existence of high inflation with high unemployment is known as Stagflation.

The Phillips curve had observed an inverse relationship between inflation and unemployment. Keynes had stated that inflation generally occur beyond the level of full employment. But stagflation proved that Phillips curve hypothesis was wrong.

Causes of Stagflation:
  ➢ Keynesian Approach
  ➢ Monetary Economist Approach
  ➢ Supply Side Economist

(1) Keynesian Approach:
    Keynes argues that increase in the cost of production (cost-push inflation) is responsible for stagflation. The cost increases due to hike in oil prices, wage increases due to strong trade unions and changes in the composition of demand for labour in the dynamic economy. The combined result of these forces is to create stagflationary pressure in the economy.

(2) Monetary Economist Approach:
    According to monetary economist (Monetarist) the phenomenon of stagflation is the result of changes in inflationary expectation. In the long run the expansionary monetary policy will lead to an increase in both price level and rate of unemployment.

(3) Supply Side Economist:
    According to the supply side economists stagflation is the result of various

government regulations, control action that restrict production and aggregate supply. Reduction in aggregate supply is responsible for stagflation.

The important cause of stagflation is found in reduction in aggregate supply. As a result there is a rise in price level and decline in employment. We can explain stagflation with the help of following figure:-

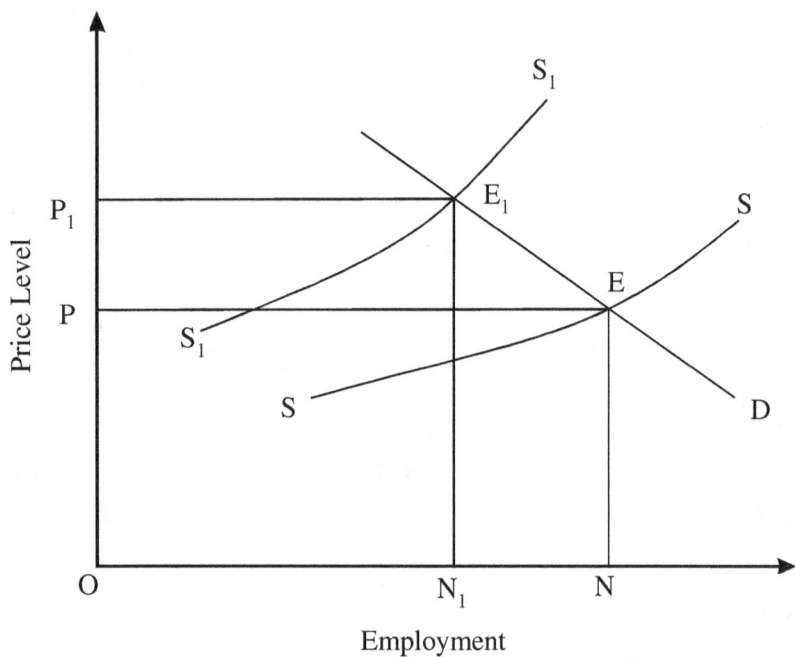

Employment

The phenomenon of stagflation is illustrated in the above diagram where employment is measured on the horizontal axis and the price level on the vertical axis. D is the aggregate demand curve. SS and SS1 are the aggregate supply curve. The initial equilibrium is at point E where aggregate demand curve intersect aggregate supply curve. The price level is OP and the employment level is ON. Now there is reduction in aggregate supply and supply curve shift upward from SS to SS1. This new supply curve intersect demand curve at point E1. As a result there is an increase in price level from OP to OP1 and reduction in employment level from ON to ON1. In this way due to reduction in aggregate supply there is rise in price level and unemployment. Hence stagflation refers to a simultaneous growth of inflation and unemployment. Government must adopt proper fiscal measures and monetary policy to reduce unemployment.

_____

QUESTIONS

1) What do you understand by the term inflation?
2) What is Stagflation?
3) What is Cost push inflation?
4) What is Demand pull inflation?
5) What are the causes of inflation?
6) Define inflation and discuss various types of inflation.
7) What is Deflation? Explain the causes and effects of deflation.
8) Explain in detail the concept of Inflationary Gap.
9) Explain the Phillips Curve. What is the trade off in the short run?
10) Explain fully the concept of Demand pull inflation and Cost push inflation.
11) What is Phillips Curve?
12) What are the consequences or effects of inflation?
13) Write a note on inflationary gap.
14) Write explanatory note on : Phillip's Curve.

<table>
<tr><td>

Chapter 6

</td><td>

TRADE CYCLE

</td></tr>
</table>

CONTENTS

INTRODUCTION

The trade cycles are the ups and downs in the economic activities. Trade cycles are fluctuation in the aggregate economic activity and therefore are concerned with the economy as a whole. The cyclical changes have attracted the major attention of economists as they affect the economic development and their causes can not be easily found out. During the last several hundred years, economists, philosophers, stock brokers and common man have tried to give various causes of business cycles.

6.1   MEANING, DEFINITION AND FEATURES OF TRADE CYCLE

Trade cycle or Business cycle is a part of the capitalist economy. There are upward and downward movement in business which is called as trade cycle. The term "Trade Cycle" in economics refers to the wave like fluctuations in the aggregate economic activity particularly in employment, output and income. In other words, trade cycle have upswing and downswing in the economic activity. Economic activity expands when the forces of expansion are in operation. Alternatively, the forces of contraction lead to the all out contraction of the economy. These phases of expansion and contraction in economic activity appear to have alternated in the economic history of capitalist countries. The cyclical pattern of these fluctuations in economic activity is known as trade cycle or business cycle.

The term 'trade cycle' has been defined in various ways by different economists. Some definitions of trade cycle are as under:

I. Keynes define trade cycle as "A trade cycle is composed of periods of good trade characterized by rising prices and low unemployment percentages altering with period of bad trade characterized by falling prices and high unemployment percentages."

II. According to Hoberler, "The trade cycle in the general sense may be defined as an alternation of period of prosperity and depression of good and bad trade."

III. Prof. Gardon defines it as, "Business cycles consist of recurring alternations of expansion and contracting in aggregate economic activity, the alternating movement in each direction being self reinforcing and pervading virtually, all parts of the economy."

IV. According to Prof. Schumpeter "A trade cycle represents wave-like deviations in business activity from the equilibrium or trend line of the economy caused by outside impulses operating upon the economy."

V. According to Hicks "Cyclical fluctuations are movements of the system above and below the rising trend or growth line."

In short business cycle is an alternate expansion and contraction in the overall business activity.

Features of trade cycle or business cycle are as follows:

The main characteristics of trade cycle may be stated as follows:

1. Business cycle operates periodically.

2. Expansion and contraction in a trade cycle are cumulative in effect.

3. A business cycle is a wave like movement of aggregate economic activities of a nation.

4. Trade cycle is characterized by upward and downward movements.

5. The cyclical fluctuations in business cycle are recurrent in nature. In every occurrence of the cycle, there is an order, regularity of expansion or contraction of economic activities.

6. These fluctuations occur in aggregate variable such as aggregate output, aggregate income, aggregate employment and prices.

7. Trade cycle relates to ups and downs in all the economic activities and not only to ups and downs in a particular industry or firm. It means that the variations are universal and affecting all the sectors of the economy.

8. Trade cycle is an international phenomenon. Different countries of the world have trade relations. Hence, a trade cycle started in a nation spreads in the other nations.

6.2 PHASES OF TRADE CYCLE

A trade cycle is commonly divided in to four phases:-
➢ Prosperity
➢ Recession
➢ Depression
➢ Recovery

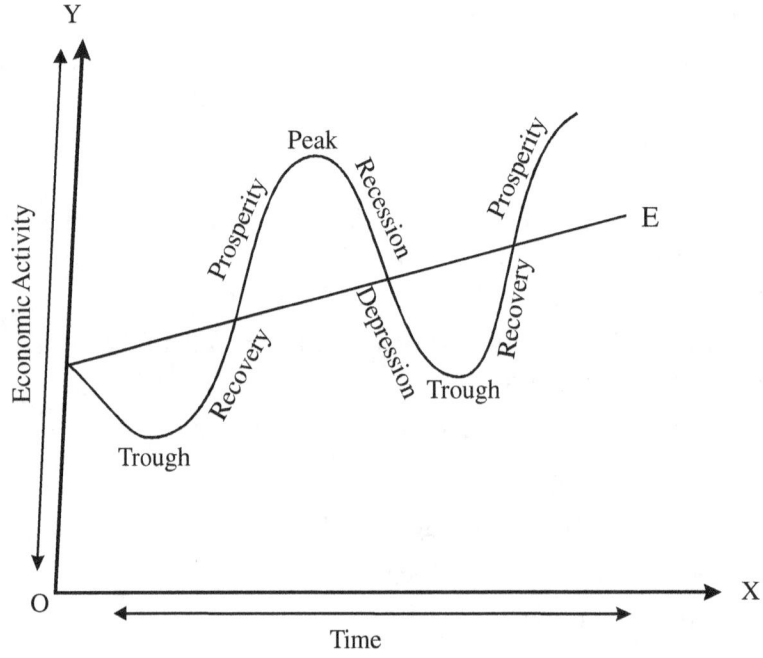

Phases of the Trade Cycle

In the above diagram, the time period is shown on the x axis and the level of economic activity on the y axis. It must be noted that the highest level of economic activity is represent by the Peak while the lowest level of economic activity occurs in the Trough. Normal level of the economic activity is shown by the horizontal line. Any deviation from this level shows the business fluctuations. The four phases of business cycle or trade cycle are explained as follows:

1) Prosperity:

Prosperity is the most desirable stage of trade cycle. This phase is also known as expansion or upswing. There is an overall atmosphere of optimism. During this phase all the economic activities have upward trends. Prof. Haberler defines prosperity as "a state of affairs in which the real income consumed, real income produced and level of employment rising and there is no idle resources or unemployed workers."

The important features of prosperity are as under:

a) A rise in price level.
b) A high level of output.
c) High level of effective demand.
d) An increase in the level of employment.
e) A high level of income.
f) A large expansion of bank credit.
g) Overall business optimism.
h) High price, high profit, a high rate of formation of new business and full employment.

The Peak or Prosperity may lead the economy to over full employment and to inflationary rise in prices. It is a symptom of the end of the prosperity phase and the beginning of the recession.

2) Recession

The economy goes at a rapid rate from prosperity to depression. So it is also called as 'Upper turning point'. When prosperity ends the recession starts. This phase is relatively short or temporary. During recession there is pessimistic atmosphere in the economy. There is reduction in investment during recession. The prices start falling due to the excess of supply over demand. There is an increase in unemployment. There is reduction in income level and reduction in effective demand. There is contraction in bank credit. The stock market experiences downfall. There is an increase in liquidity preference. Recession has a cumulative effect. This crisis ultimately results in depression.

3) Depression

Depression is the most undesirable phase of a trade cycle. During depression there is an overall reduction in aggregate economic activity. The important features of depression are as under:-

a) Reduction in aggregate demand.
b) Fall in price level.
c) Reduction in income level.
d) Reduction in volume of output and trade.
e) Reduction in consumption expenditure.
f) Unemployment increases.
g) Contraction of bank credit.

A depression cannot be regarded as a permanent feature of the economy. After sometime there will be a moderate increase in the demand for goods and services. This will lead to an increase in production, increase in employment, income and aggregate effective demand. Therefore a stage of recovery starts.

4) Recovery or Revival Phase

This phase is known as lower turning point from depression to prosperity. Recovery implies increase in business activity after the lowest point of the depression. During this phase there is an improvement in economic activity when the demand for consumer goods increases it leads to increase in the demand for capital goods. There is an increase in investment, increase in employment and income which leads to further rise in demand. During recovery phase level of employment, output and income slowly and steadily improve. Business activities go on expanding and recovery takes place. The recovery phase continues until the level of business activity is same as it was before the decline. The more severe the depression, the more rapid is the recovery.

6.3 POLICY FOR CONTROL OF TRADE CYCLE- MONETARY AND FISCAL MEASURES

Business cycles create business fluctuations in economic activities of the capitalist economy and hamper the sooth and orderly progress of the society. Hence the efforts have to be made to control them.

In modern times, a programme of economic stabilization is usually directed towards the attainment of three objective- (i) Encouraging and sustaining economic growth at full employment level. (ii) Maintaining the value of money through price stabilization. (iii) Controlling cyclical fluctuations.

The following measures are used to control trade cycle:
➢ Monetary Policy
➢ Fiscal Policy

Monetary Policy

Trade cycle once originates, it is always aggravated by the monetary factors. Monetary inflation leads to higher prices and higher profits. It induces business and entrepreneurs to make investment on account of optimistic climate, business activities tend to flourish rapidly and upswing of the cycle takes place. On the contrary, monetary deflation leads to lower prices, lower profits and widespread pessimistic outlook, which leads to the downswing of the cycle. Hence the government has to evolve a suitable monetary policy to control the trade cycles in the economy.

Monetary policy is implemented through the central bank of the country,

The central bank uses qualitative and quantitative measures for controlling credit in the economy. The quantitative measures include I) Bank Rate or Discount Rate Policy II) Open market operations. III) Variable Cash Reserve Ratio. Let us discuss them briefly.

I) Bank Rate Policy -

Bank rate is a traditional weapon of credit control used by central bank. The bank rate is the official minimum rate at which the central bank of a country is prepared to rediscount approved bill of exchange. But for all practical purpose the bank rate is taken as the rate at which the R.B.I. extends loans & advances to the commercial banks. The commercial banks decide their interest rate based on the bank rate of the central bank. During the period of prosperity, inflationary tendencies tend to become dominant. Hence the central bank raises the bank rate. As a result the borrowing from central bank becomes costly, which discourages the commercial banks to borrow from the central bank. The commercial banks in turn raise their lending rates to the business community and hence the borrowers tend to borrow less from the commercial banks. This results in contraction of credit in the economy and prices are checked from rising further. On the other hand, during depression when the general prices level is depressed, the central bank lowers the bank rate and correspondingly commercial banks also lower their lending rates to the business community. So the businessmen and entrepreneurs are encouraged to borrow more and invest in profitable ventures. Thus the employment, output and income start rising and the downward trend of price level is checked.

II) Open Market Operations -

Open market operation refer to the sale and purchase of the securities in money market by the central bank. During the period of propensity when the prices are rising, the central bank sells securities, which tends to reduce money supply in the economy. As the cash reserves of commercial banks are reduced, their capacity to create credit is reduced hence borrowing from commercial banks tends to be discouraged and rising price level is checked. When recessionary tendencies prevail in the economy the central bank buys securities. This leads to the increase in the cash reserves of the commercial banks, so they tend to lend more to the business community and entrepreneurs which results in increase in investment that in turn leads to the increase in output, employment and income. As demand rises the decline in the price level is checked.

III) Variable Reserve Ratio-

Variable Reserve Ratio as a method of credit control was suggested by Keynes. This method was introduced by Federal Reserve System of USA in 1935. A variation in reserve requirement influences a banker's ability to create credit. There are two types of Reserve Ratio:-
   (1) Cash Reserve Ratio (CRR)
   (2) Statutory Liquidity Ratio (SLR)

Cash Reserve Ratio refers to the portion of total deposits of a commercial bank which it has to keep with the central bank in the form of cash.

Statutory Liquidity Ratio refers to that portion of total deposit of a commercial bank which is required to keep in the form of gold and other government securities.

The method of variable reserve ratio is more direct and more effective method of credit control. This method is comparatively new method of credit control. In India the Reserve Bank of India fixes the cash reserve ratio from time to time.

During inflation the central bank increases cash reserve ratio which adversely affect of credit creation capacity of commercial bank. As a result money supply and price level decline. Hence during inflation central bank adopt contraction of credit method.

During depression the central bank reduce cash reserve ratio which leads to expansion of credit creation capacity. As a result money supply increases. Hence during depression central bank adopt expansion of credit method.

Qualitative or Selective Measures:

The quantitative measures are to regulate total volume of credit in the economy whereas qualitative or selective measures are used for controlling the use, direction and distribution of credit. Following are different weapons of selective measures:

(I) Margin Requirement:

Commercial banks provide loan on the basis of some security. A commercial bank does not advance loan to the full amount of the security. The margin requirement is the difference between the market value of the security and its loan value. The gap between the loan amount and the value of security is called as "margin". The Central bank directs the commercial banks to fix margin requirement. Commercial bank provides credit on the basis of security. If a security has a market value of Rs.100000/- and if the margin requirement is 30 percent then the maximum loan that can be advanced by bank is Rs. 70000/-

An increase in the margin requirement will reduce the amount of loan. The central bank may ask commercial bank to keep higher margins while providing loan against stock of food grains, sugar, groundnut etc.

Margin requirement is a simple method of credit control and can be easily administered.

(II) Regulation of consumer credit:

The second instrument of selective credit control is the regulation of consumer credit. This method was first introduced in USA in 1941. Durable consumer goods are sold on hire purchase basis or on installment basis. Consumer get loan from bank for installment buying. The commercial bank provides credit to consumer to buy durable goods such as Refrigerator, television, furniture, washing machine etc. The regulation of consumer credit consists of rules regarding down payment and maximum period of installment. This method is an extremely useful for controlling inflation and maintaining economic stability. During inflationary condition the consumer credit is controlled through higher interest rates, more downpayments and less installment whereas during depression or recession low interest rate, less downpayment and more installments are applied to increase demand for goods and services.

(III) Rationing of credit:

Rationing of credit is a selective method adopted by the central bank for controlling and regulating the purpose for which credit is allocated by commercial banks.

Credit rationing may be introduced in two ways (1) The Central bank may impose a ceiling on the aggregate or maximum amount of loans and advances made by every commercial bank which is called as variable portfolio ceiling (quota). (2) The Central bank fixes a ratio between the capital of a bank and the value of its total assets. This method is called as variable capital asset ratio. Both this methods of credit rationing are quantitative as well as qualitative in effect.

(IV) Moral Suasion:

Moral suasion refers to requesting or persuading commercial banks to follow a particular policy or not. This method is purely informal. Moral suasion is a psychological means of controlling credit. The Central bank may also appeal to the banks to follow the general monetary policy. The Central bank may request commercial banks not to obtain further recommendation from itself or not to use the accommodation already obtained for speculative purpose.

During depression commercial banks may be persuaded to expand their volume of loans and advances whereas during inflation the Central bank may request commercial banks to keep away from financing speculation and non-essential activities.

(V) Direct Action:

Direct legal action is the final effort by the central bank to make the commercial banks follow the credit control measures. Direct actions are taken by Central bank by issuing specific directives, charging a penal rate of interest for commercial banks borrowing from central bank and by canceling the license of the commercial bank.

(VI) Publicity:

The Central bank periodically publishes review, reports and statements regarding business conditions, money market, banking condition and so on. Publicity is one of the functions of Central bank. Through publicity commercial banks, traders, businessman and common public gets idea and knowledge about the overall policy of the central bank.

The above all qualitative measures are particularly useful in developing countries.

Fiscal Policy

Fiscal Policy is that part of government economic policy, that deals with taxation, expenditure and management of public debt in the economy. Fiscal policy measures are undertaken by Ministry of Finance, and it is implemented through the income and expenditure of the government. It is often used as a technique to attain and maintain full employment by manipulating the government budget. According to Lerner's concept of "Functional Finance", fiscal policy should be contra-cyclical in nature and should be used for economic stabilization. Keynes advocated unbalanced budget policy in the short run to achieve economic stability and full employment.

The main instruments of fiscal policy include taxation, government expenditure and public debt, which can be used to control trade cycles in a capitalist economy more effectively. Let us study how these measures are used.

I) Taxation -

Taxation is a powerful instrument in the hands of public authorities to bring about changes in disposable incomes, consumption and investment. During the propensity phase of business cycle inflationary tendencies are dominant and price rise is widespread in the economy. In order to control inflation it is necessary to reduce the size of disposable income in the hands of the public because of limited supply of goods and services in the market. In order to take away the excess purchasing power from the public, the level of existing taxation is raised and new taxes may be imposed on goods & services so that money supply with the public will be reduced. Thus inflation can be brought under control to some extent. During depression, it is necessary to step up, both, consumption and investment in the economy. Hence commodity taxes should be reduced so as to stimulate consumption and reduction in corporate and business taxes helps in stimulating investment in the economy. Progressive taxation may be used to redistribute income and promote consumption.

II) Public expenditure -

Public expenditure relates to variations in government spending on goods & services to effect changes in the level of aggregate demand. During prosperity aggregate effective demand rises rapidly on account of increase in private expenditure. To counteract increase in private expenditure the government should reduce its expenditure to the minimum possible level, so as to control an aggregate demand to some extent.

During depression, on account of recessionary trends effective demand declines significantly. Hence it is necessary to increase government expenditure to compensate decline in private expenditure. Increase in government expenditure tends to increase purchasing power with the public, which tend to increase effective demand in the economy. Rise in consumption expenditure stimulates demand for consumption goods, which in turn, stimulates demand for capital goods. It leads to increase in private investment, which in turn tends to increase income, output and employment in the economy.

III) Public Debt. -

Public debt or pubic borrowing attempts to influence the level of aggregate spending through changes in the liquid asset position. During prosperity to control inflation it is necessary to take away the excess purchasing power from the public. Public borrowing may be voluntary or compulsory. Voluntary public borrowing is generally not much effective; hence the government has to resort to compulsory borrowing from the public, such as deferred pay. According to this scheme, a certain percentage of wages and salaries of employees in compulsorily deducted in exchange of saving bonds which mature after some time. This measure is adopted to control inflation as and when needed.

During depression effective demand declines with the business recession, hence it is necessary to stimulate consumption by increasing purchasing power with the public. Redemption of public debt during depression tends to increase purchasing power with the public, which in turn stimulates effective demand in the economy and stimulate investment to achieve full employment.

According to Keynes, during period of prosperity a government should follow a policy of surplus budget by reducing its expenditure and during depression it should follow deficit budget policy in stead of following annually balanced budget policy.

Built in stabilizers

There are certain built in stabilizers or automatic stabilizers in the economy like corporate profits tax, income tax, excise duties; unemployment insurance and unemployment relief payments which tend to vary with the changes in the national income. When the tax structure remains constant, tax yields vary directly with movements in national income, while government expenditure vary inversely with the changes in national income. However the effectiveness of built in stabilizers depends on elasticity of tax receipt, level of taxes and flexibility of government expenditures. The fact is that the elasticity of tax receipt is not so high to act as automatic stabilizer, even in developed countries. These built in stabilizers are not much effective in controlling business cycles.

Discretionary Fiscal Policy

It is the policy that requires deliberate changes in the budget through changes in either taxation or government expenditure or both. However the discretionary fiscal policy depends on proper timing and accurate forecasting, which is rather difficult in practice. There are decision and execution lags, which tend to make discretionary fiscal policy ineffective in controlling business cycles. Introduction of discretionary stabilisers tends to strengthen the built-in-Stabilisers. It should be noted that a suitable mix of built-in-Stabilizer and discretionary measures should be adopted. Government expenditure on public works projects to boost aggregate demand is an example of discretionary action.

As compared to monetary policy, fiscal policy is considered as a more effective weapon to control business cycles. Monetary policy tends to be effective in developed countries whereas fiscal policy is relatively more effective in developing countries. However the combination of both the policies, which tends to be mutually reinforcing is considered as a desirable measure for controlling business cycles. In recovery from depression, the deficit financing may play a larger role, both by creating new income directly and by helping to implement an easy money policy. While in a boom, monetary policy would play an important and perhaps even the predominant role.

_____

QUESTIONS

1) Define a Trade Cycle.
2) State the various features of Trade Cycle.
3) What is Depression?
4) What is Recession?
5) What is Monetary Policy?
6) Define Fiscal Policy.
7) Describe the various Phases of Trade Cycle.
8) What is Trade Cycle? Explain the various Phases of Trade Cycle in detail.
9) Outline in detail the Anti-cyclical measures.
10) Discuss the various policies to control the occurrence of Trade Cycle.
11) What are Anti-Cyclical Fiscal Measures?
12) Explain the meaning and features of Trade Cycle.

Chapter 7 | THEORIES OF OUTPUT AND EMPLOYMENT

CONTENTS

INTRODUCTION

Keynes was the first economist who developed systematic theory of employment in his book 'The General Theory of Employment, Interest and Money' which was published in 1936. There are two important theories for the determination of the level of income and employment (1) The Classical Theory of Employment and (2) Keynesian Theory of Employment. Keynes has used the term of classical theory in a broad sense. The term Classical theory was used by him to denote the thoughts of classical economists like Adam Smith, Ricardo, J.B. Says, Marx and neo-classical economists like Marshall, Pigou etc. on employment.

7.1 CLASSICAL THEORIES OF EMPLOYMENT – SAYS, PIGOU

Classical Theory of Employment

The Classical theory of employment is based on the assumption that there is a natural tendency of the economy to achieve and maintain full employment equilibrium in the long run and any deviations from full employment is temporary and abnormal phenomena. The classical theory of employment is based on the following assumptions.

i) There exists full employment without inflation.
ii) There is a free market price system. The forces of supply and demand interact in the market and determine market price.

iii) There is perfect competition both in commodity market and factor market
iv) There is a closed Laissez faire economy i.e. government intervention is minimum.
v) Labour is homogenous
vi) Wages and prices are flexible
vii) Total output of the economy is divided into consumption and investment expenditures.
viii) The quantity of money is given.
ix) Since Say's Law prevails, i.e. supply creates its own demand, there can never be deficiency in demand.
x) Money wages and real wages are directly related and proportional.
xi) Capital stock and technological knowledge remain constant in the short run.

The classical economists concentrated on the study of growth of the economy from long run point of view and the efficient allocation of resources at the level of full employment, so they concentrated on the supply side of economic growth. They assumed that full employment of the factors of production as a normal situation in the long run, and any deviation from this condition was temporary and abnormal. They believed that, under perfect competition, in a free enterprise capitalist economy, free forces of supply and demand operate through a free market system which tend to maintain full employment without inflation, and the full employment output in produced through the optimum use of the resources in the long run. Hence they concentrated upon production of different types of good and services, optimum allocation of resources, relative price structure of different goods and services produced and distribution of real income among the factors of production in the economy. The Classical belief in full employment was based upon the operation of Say's law of markets, and wages price flexibility.

Say's Law of Markets

J.B.Say, French Economist, in early 19th Century developed a proposition that "Supply creates its own demand", which is known as the Say's Law of markets. Initially he considered a barter economy where goods are exchanged for goods. Supply of a good under barter system is the direct source of demand for some other commodity; supply of goods and services generates an equivalent demand for other goods and services. Even in money economy, producers use the factors of production as inputs for producing goods and services. During the process of production factors of production are rewarded in terms of rent, interest, wages & profit. These payments create demand for goods and services produced in the economy. As whole of the income is spent on purchasing goods and services, whatever is produced is sold. Hence there is no overproduction and aggregate supply tends to be exactly equal to the aggregate demand at the level of the economy as a whole. There may be over production of a particular commodity because of inaccurate estimate of the quantity of it required by others. But such deviation can be adjusted by reducing production of it. Thus supply creates its own demand. Accordingly, Say's law of markets is a denial of the possibility of general over production, that is, a denial of possibility of a deficiency of aggregate demand. Therefore the employment of more resources will always be profitable and will take place to the point of full employment, subject to the limitation on that the contributors of resources are willing to accept rewards no greater than their physical unemployment, according to this view, if workers will accept what they are worth.

Assumptions of Say's Law of Market :

i) There is a free exchange economy where there is perfect freedom for sellers to sell and buyers to buy. Perfect competition prevails in the economy and there are no restrictions imposed either on producers or consumers and the free market forces determine the equilibrium price and output

ii) There is free flow of money income and all the income received by the owners of the factors of production are immediately spent either on consumption or saving which are automatically invested. Thus there is an equality between savings and investment.

iii) The equality between the savings and investment is brought about by flexible interest rate.

iv) The Government follows the policy of "laissez faire" or non-interference in the free play of market forces of supply and demand.

v) The size of market is limited by the volume of production, so that supply creates its own demand.

vi) There is a closed economy and external force does not affect its automatic functioning in any way.

Implications of Say's Law.

On the basis of the discussion of say's law its implications may be stated as follows :

i) Automatic Functioning of the Economic system

The economic system is self-adjusting and functions automatically without direction of any controlling authority. If there is any disequilibrium it tends to be temporary and free market forces operate to bring about equilibrium. For example, if demand increases, then price will increase, so that supply will increase and extra demand may be satisfied. Thus there is a built in flexibility.

ii) Impossibility of General overproduction

According to Say's law general over production is not possible because, whenever there is overproduction, prices will fall and demand will increase, so that the surplus stock will be cleared. There may be overproduction at the level of particular industry but it will be a temporary phenomenon and necessary adjustments will take place automatically. In a free and fully competitive system there will not be either over-production or underproduction. As J.S.Mill has pointed out, "Whatever the amount of the annual produce, it can never exceed the amount of annual demand," As production increase factor incomes also increase and thus the new demand is created and increased stock, will be sold in the market.

Circular Flow of Income

The flow of income in the economy can be explained with the help of a circular flow of income.

When the firms employ the factors of production, they are remunerated in terms of rent wages and interest. The owners of the factors of production are the households who receive this income. Households spend this income for purchasing the goods and services produced and supplied by the firms. It is assumed that all the income earned is spent either on consumption or saved and all the saving in the economy are automatically invested. Thus the flow of income that is generated in the economy can be explained with the help of a diagram as follows.

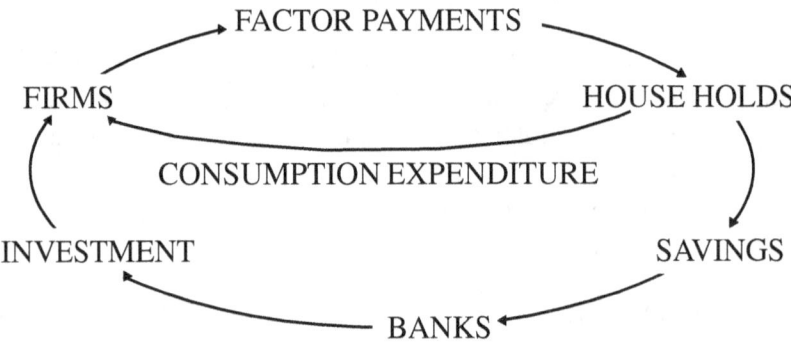

iii) Impossibility of General unemployment

Under free and perfectly competitive economic system general unemployment is also not possible. As Pigou has argued a general reduction in wages would create enough demand for labour to remove unemployment. There should not be interference like wage regulation by government or trade union pressure to resist wages. There will be a natural tendency towards attaining full employment in the long run. Unemployment may exist in case of a particular industry but general unemployment is not possible in the long run.

iv) Employment of unemployed resources will pay its own way

When unemployed resources are employed, they will help in producing more output, as a result national income will increase and it becomes possible to pay the newly employed resources out of it. Thus the community has not to suffer loss but it gains by employing unemployed resources.

v) Laissez faire Policy of the Government

An important policy implication of Say's Law is that, the government should follow Laissez faire (let alone) policy and it should not interfere in economic activities. Any interference by the government may result into disequilibria and imbalance. According to J.B.Say the economic system is automatic or self-adjusting. It can work itself without any external stimulus. It has built in flexibility. Even if any obstacle arises the system gets over it in due course of time. Hence the government should not interfere with the working of the economic system and leave prices wages and interest rates free to adjust themselves to the changing situations.

vi) No Limit to Productive Activities.

According to J.B.Say supply creates its own demand. There is no limit to productive activities in the economy. It implies that, economic development can take place to any extent, as there can be no deficiency of effective demand. Thus developing countries have unlimited scope for economic development.

vii) Neutral Role of Money

The law is based on the assumption that there is a barter economy where goods are exchanged for goods. Thus corresponding to the flow of money income there is a flow of goods and services. Money is just a medium of exchange and changes in supply of money has no effect on the process of equilibrium in the real economy at the level of full employment.

CRITICISM OF SAY'S LAW

Keynes and others have criticized Say's Law of markets on the following grounds.

i) Supply does not create its own demand.

According to Say's law production creates demand for goods produced,hence supply creates its own demand. But it is based on the assumption that, the people spend their entire income on the purchase of goods. But in modern economies, people do not spend their entire income and save a part of it, for future use. This saving reduces the present demand for goods and hence some part of present production remains unsold. The saving serves as a leakage and reduces the flow of income in the economics, Hence deficiency in aggregate demand leads to overproduction in the economy.

It was argued that, even though part of income is saved, it is converted into investment and hence there would be no deficiency of demand. But this is based on assumption that the rate of interest plays an important role in bringing about equality between savings and investment. The fact is the main determinant of investment is not the rate of interest but the expectation of profit and hence there is no guarantee that the saving will always be equal to investment, and savings may result into deficiency of demand.

ii) Absence of self-adjustment

According to Say's Law full employment is maintained by automatic and self-adjusting mechanism in the long run. But Keynes emphasized that unemployment cannot be removed by automatic mechanism and it can only be removed by increasing the rate of investment.

iii) Possibility of Overproduction

Say's law stated that supply creates its own demand and hence general overproduction does not take place. Keynes argued that, all the income received by the factors of production is not spent and part of it is saved which may not be automatically invested. Hence savings and investment are not always equal. This inequality leads to overproduction and unemployment.

iv) Money does not play neutral role

Say's law of markets is mainly based on a barter system, so it neglects the role of money in the system. Keynes emphasized the role of money as a medium of exchange and people hold money as income and for business motives. Thus money does not play a neutral role.

v) Underemployment Equilibrium

Keynes held that underemployment equilibrium is a normal condition in a capitalist system, while full employment is a special case. Generally supply tends to be more than the demand, which gives rise to unemployment.

vi) Equality through income

Classical economists believed that, the equality between saving and investment is brought about through the mechanism of interest rate. Keynes demonstrated that it is the level of income, which brings about this equality and not by the rate of interest.

vii) Wage cut is not the solution

Pigou advised wage cut policy to solve the problem of unemployment, which may be true at micro level. Keynes held that wage cut policy tends to increase unemployment due to fall in effective demand and the trade unions tend to resist such policy. Hence instead of flexible wage policy, flexible monetary policy is the desirable solution to solve the problem of unemployment.

viii) State intervention is necessary

Say's Law is based on the assumption of the laissez fair policy. But this is the policy, which leads to unemployment and overproduction in the economy. Keynes advocated state intervention for adjusting aggregate supply and aggregate demand in the economy through fiscal and monetary measures.

ix) Demand creates its own supply

Keynes criticized the proposition that supply creates its own demand and emphasized exactly opposite view that demand creates its own supply. Unemployment is the result of lack of effective demand as people do not spend all of their income on consumption and part of it is generally saved.

x) Neutral Role of Money

The classical economists believed that money is merely a medium of exchange. They neglected the role of money affecting income, output and employment.

PIGOU- 'WAGE-CUT POLICY'

Pigou, one of the foremost Classical economist, favoured the policy of 'wage cuts' to solve the problem of unemployment. According to Pigou, "With perfectly free competition, there will always be at work a strong tendency for wage rates to be so related to demand that everybody is employed." Thus if prices and wages are allowed to vary freely without any interference then unemployment would soon disappear and full employment will be restored in course of time. It is the flexibility of wages and prices which automatically brings about full employment in the economy. For example, if there is general overproduction resulting in depression and unemployment prices will fall, so that the demand will increase, which in turn lead to increase in prices and productive activities in the economy and hence unemployment would tend to disappear. Similarly, whenever there is unemployment, it could be removed by cutting down wage. When wages are reduced then demand for labour will increase and the economic activities in the economy will increase rapidly.

Keynes objected Pigou's formulation that a cut in money wages could achieve full employment in the economy. This may hold good at the micro level but it is not applicable at the macro level or aggregate level. If money wages are reduced for all the workers in the country, then it will reduce purchasing power with the people, which in turn reduce effective demand in the economy. This results in overproduction and unemployment.

Keynes strongly opposed Piou's view that unemployment would disappear, if there was general cut in wages. According to Keynes, this wage cut will fail to bring about increases in employment because it will mainly cause a reduction in aggregate demand. The wage-cut policy will leave less purchasing power in the hands of workers leading to fall in demand which ultimately will reduce the volume of employment. It will deepen the depression. Pigou's effect or the real balance effect has no relevance as a guide to policy. The Classical theory of employment was rejected by Keynes both on theoretical and practical ground.

Keynes did not favour a flexible wage policy in the form of a cut in money wages on certain practical ground. According to him, such a policy would be opposed by trade unions. They would not accept an all-round reduction in money wages. In democratic countries, where collective bargaining is permissible, reduction in money wages is an impracticable possibility. Therefore it is much easier to follow a flexible monetary policy than a flexible wage policy. So Keynes recommended use of fiscal and monetary policy to overcome the problem of unemployment.

7.2 KEYNESIAN CRITICISM ON CLASSICAL THEORIES OF EMPLOYMENT

Keynes criticized classical theory of output and employment and explained its limitations as follows.

i) Unrealistic Assumption of full employment

Keynes argued that the assumption of full employment is unrealistic; the general tendency in a capitalist economy is that of underemployment equilibrium, because the economy does not function according to the Say's law and excess supply over its demand is the normal situation. The existence of involuntary unemployment proves that underemployment equilibrium is a normal condition while full employment equilibrium is an accidental or abnormal situation.

ii) Keynes rejected Say's Law of Market

Keynes rejected the Say's Law of Markets i.e. supply creates its own demand. He argued that all the income earned by the owners of factors of production is not spent for purchasing goods and services produced by them. A part of income is saved, which is not automatically invested. This results in a deficiency of aggregate demand and overproduction in the economy. As whatever is produced cannot be sold, general unemployment is its result.

iii) Outdated laissez faire policy

Keynes rejected the classical view that the laissez faire policy is essential or an automatic and self-adjusting process of full employment equilibrium. Keynes argued that the capitalist structure of society is not self-adjusting and automatic in nature. The capitalist society is divided into two classes of rich and poor. The rich people are so rich that they cannot spend all of their income on consumption while poor people do not have income to purchase goods and services required by them. As a result there is general deficiency of effective demand, which leads to overproduction and unemployment, leading to depression, Keynes advocated state intervention for adjusting the forces of supply and demand in the economy through monetary and fiscal measures.

iv) Rate of Interest is not a Strategic Variable

The classical economists believed that savings and investment are equal at the level of full employment and if any divergence arises then the rate of interest plays a strategic role in bringing about equality between saving and investment.

Keynes argued that the level of saving depends on the level of income and not on the rate of interest. The level of investment is not only determined by the rate of interest but also by the marginal efficiency of capital. When business community is pessimistic, even the low rate of interest fails to motivate them to invest. Thus it is the level of income that determines savings and the marginal efficiency of capital determines investment where the rate of interest plays a secondary role.

v) Wage cut policy is ineffective

Keynes objected Pigou's formulation that a cut in money wages could achieve full employment in the economy. This may hold good at the micro level but it is not applicable at the aggregate or macro level. If money wages are reduced for all the workers in the country, then it will reduce purchasing power with the people, which in turn reduces effective demand in the economy. This results in overproduction and unemployment. From practical point of view, workers and their unions are not ready to accept lower wages. So Keynes recommended use of fiscal and monetary policy to overcome the problem of unemployment.

vi) Excessive Importance to the Long Period

The classical economists concentrated on the long-term full employment equilibrium through self-adjusting mechanism. Keynes argued that the long period is so long that "all of us might be dead." Long period is a series of short periods. In practice we face problems related to short run. During short period tastes and preferences of consumers, technology, supply of labour etc are constant. Assuming consumption demand to be constant he advocated increase in investment for removing unemployment.

vii) Static Approach

The classical economists concentrated on equilibrium at a certain point of time, hence it is static approach but Keynes introduces future expectations into his economic analysis and tried to analyze dynamic economy, which is more realistic approach.

Thus the classical theory of output and employment is based on unrealistic assumption. It is not capable to solve the economic problems faced, by modern complex and dynamic capitalist economies.

7.3 KEYNESIAN THEORY OF EMPLOYMENT

Keynes was the first economist who developed systematic theory of employment in his book "The General Theory of Employment, Interest and Money" which was published in 1936. According to him, in a capitalist economy the level of employment depends on effective demand. Unemployment arises due to a lack of effective demand and a deficiency of outlay on consumption and investment. Effective demand is the sole determinant of employment in Keynes theory of employment.

Principle of Effective Demand:

According to Keynes total employment in the economy depend upon effective demand. Keynes theory of employment is known as effective demand theory of employment. Unemployment arises due to deficiency of effective demand. To solve the problem of employment it is necessary to increase effective demand.

Effective Demand refers to the aggregate demand in an economy. Keynes argued that the level of income and output in the economy is determined by the level of employment and the level of employment itself is determined by the level of effective demand. Effective demand depends on the total spending of the community. If community decide to spend on the purchase of consumption goods as well as on purchase of capital goods or investment goods then

Effective Demand = C+I

But today government spending which has become as important part of total spending and hence

Effective Demand = C+I+G

Where C = Consumption Expenditure

I = Investment Expenditure

G = Government Expenditure on consumption and investment goods

According to Keynes effective demand is determined by two factors:-

➢ Aggregate Supply Function (ASF)
➢ Aggregate Demand Function (ADF)

Aggregate Supply Function (ASF)

Aggregate Supply Function can be defined as "A schedule which show the minimum expected receipts for different levels of output and employment." Aggregate supply is nothing but the cost of production which must be recovered by the entrepreneur. The Supply price for any given quantity of commodity refers to that price at which the seller is willing to supply that commodity in the market. The minimum proceeds at a particular level of employment is called the Aggregate Supply Price (ASP).

At different level of employment there is different Aggregate Supply Price. There is direct relationship between employment and aggregate supply price which is presented in the following Aggregate Supply Schedule:-

Aggregate Supply Schedule

Level of employment (N) (in lakhs of workers)	Aggregate Supply Price (Rs. in Crores)
1	100
2	200
3	300
4	400
5	500
6	600

In the above schedule Aggregate Supply Price rises with the increase in the level of employment. According to Keynes the Aggregate Supply Function is an increasing function of the level of employment and can be expressed as

ASP = F (N)

ASP is the direct function of employment which can be presented graphically as follows:-

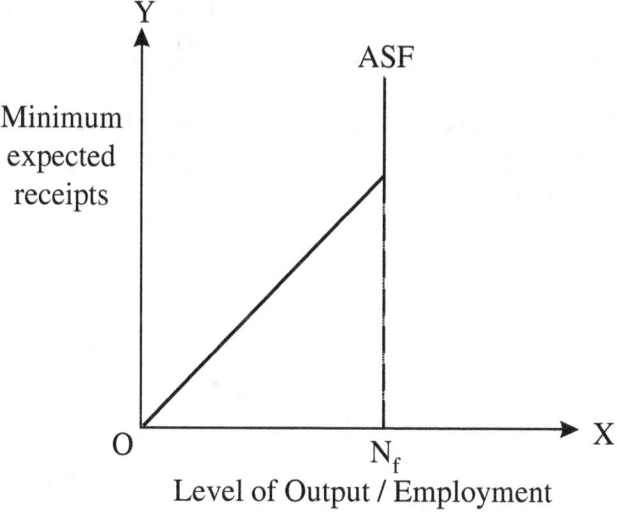

Level of Output / Employment

In the above diagram ASF curve starting from the origin slopes upward to the right as there is direct relation between employment and Aggregate supply price or cost of production. If the economy reaches at full employment there will be no further increase in employment. Hence the ASF curve becomes perfectly inelastic.

Aggregate Demand Function (ADF):-

The second important factor determining the level of effective demand is the Aggregate Demand Function (ADF).

Aggregate Demand Function (ADF) can be defined as "The maximum expected Sales receipt from different level of output." The Receipt the entrepreneur in the economy expects to obtain is called Aggregate Demand. Aggregate Demand Function is the total expenditure of the community on consumption and investment goods. It represents the total demand for goods and services. The total sum of money which is expected from the sale of the output produced by any given amount of labour employed is called the Aggregate Demand Price. There is a positive relationship between the level of employment and Aggregate Demand Price which is presented as follows:-

Aggregate Demand Schedule

Level of Employment (N) (in lakhs of workers)	Aggregate Demand Price or Expected Sales (Rs. in crores)
1	175
2	250
3	325
4	400
5	475
6	550

The Aggregate Demand Schedule states the relation between various levels of employment and the maximum sales receipt. Aggregate Demand Function may be represented graphically as follows:-

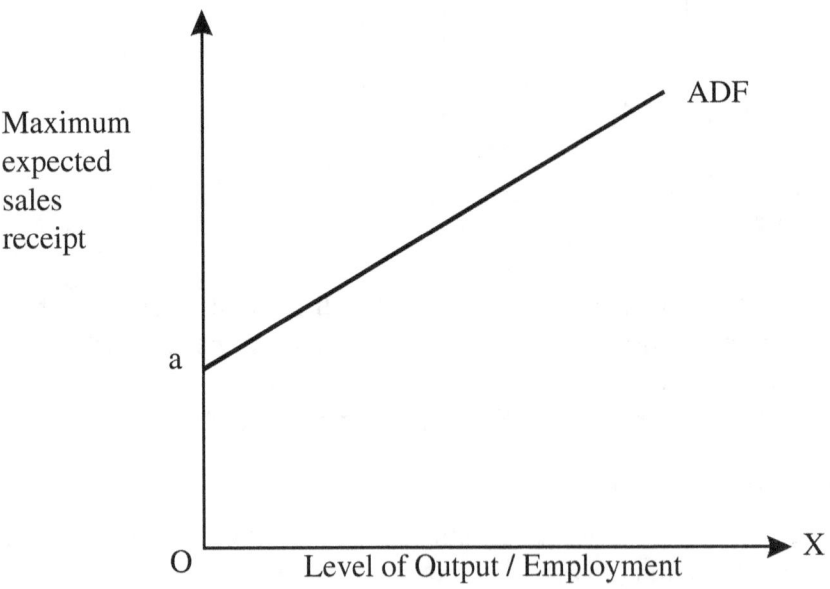

ADF curve is an upward rising curve. The ADF curve begins from the above the origin indicating that even at zero level of income there is some consumption to meet the basic minimum needs. The ADF is a positive function of the level of employment and output. As output and employment goes on increasing the expected sales receipts or Aggregate Demand Price increases.

Equilibrium level of Employment or the point of Effective Demand:-

The intersection of the aggregate demand function with the aggregate supply function determines the level of income and employment. The equilibrium level of employment in Keynes theory is determined at the level of "Effective Demand" i.e. at a point where

ASF = ADF

The ASF or Supply price represents the cost of production. The ADF represent the Revenue from sales of output or it is Aggregate demand price. The point where ASF = ADF is the point of 'Effective Demand' which determine the equilibrium level of employment and output in Keynes theory which can be presented in the following Table:-

Equilibrium level of Employment

Level of Employment (N) (in lakhs of workers)	Aggregate Supply Price (Rs. in Crores)	Aggregate Demand Price (Rs. in crores)
1	100	175
2	200	250
3	300	325
4	400	400
5	500	475
6	600	550

The economy reaches equilibrium level of employment when the aggregate demand function becomes equal to the aggregate supply function (ADF = ASF). At this point, the amount of sales proceeds which entrepreneurs expect to receive is equal to what they must receive in order to just appropriate their total costs. In the given schedule, it is Rs.400 crores which is the entrepreneur's expected minimum as well as maximum sales proceeds, so that 4 lakh workers employment is the equilibrium amount. This is the point of effective demand. This is below the full employment level indicating that in the Keynesian analysis equilibrium attain at underemployment level.
This can be presented graphically as below:

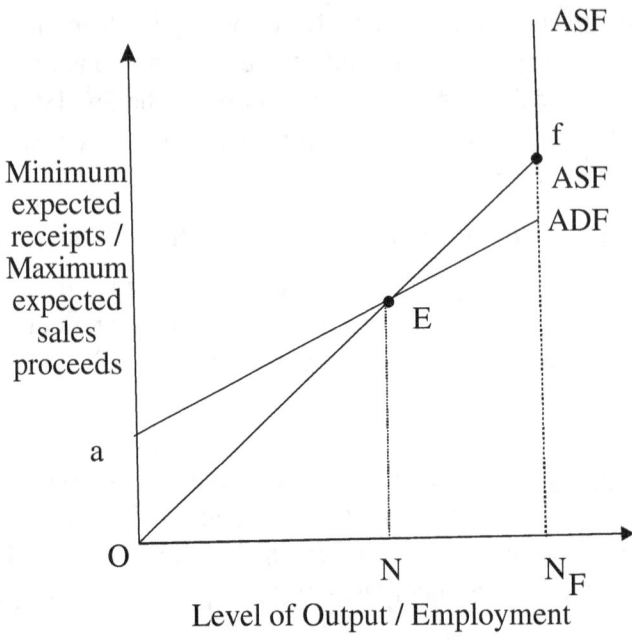

In the above diagram 'E' is the point of Effective Demand where aggregate demand curve intersect aggregate supply curve. ON is the equilibrium level of employment where **ADF = ASF**

Any number of workers more then ON can not employed because the ASF > ADF and hence entrepreneurs will incur loss. It is only at point E where ADF = ASF and normal profit maximize. Hence E is the point of effective demand and the point of equilibrium which determine the actual level of employment. But at point E economy is not in a full employment level. Hence Keynes equilibrium is at a point of less than full employment or underemployment equilibrium.

According to Keynes it is short-fall in the aggregate demand which is the main cause of unemployment in a capitalist economy. It is the ADF which is the effective element in the principle of effective demand. The principle of effective demand is the most important contribution of Keynes. It is the soul of the Keynesian theory of employment.

Criticism of the Keynesian theory of employment:-

In spite of significant contribution made by Keynes, his theory has been criticized on the following grounds:-

1) Keynes has adopted only macro economic approach. But sometimes aggregative concepts are misleading as they fail to deal with the fundamental problems faced by individual units.

2) Keynes established a direct relationship between income, output and employment. But the critics argue that employment depend on skill, invention, technique of production etc. and not alone on effective demand.

3) Keynesian theory deals with short-run. He did not explain how to solve the long-run problem of the dynamic economy.

4) Keynesian economics is mainly depression economics. It does not give attention to deal with inflationary situation.

5) The critics say that the principle of effective demand is not applicable in underdeveloped countries where the problem is of inelastic supply and not of deficiency of effective demand.

6) Keynes has not provided a comprehensive treatment of unemployment. He has concentrated on cyclical unemployment in advanced capitalist countries. He has not considered other types of unemployment, such as technological, frictional, structural etc.

7) Keynes has called his theory as General theory. But it is not applicable everywhere. Its application is limited to industrially develop and relatively rich capitalist economies like USA, UK, France etc. His theory is not applicable to underdeveloped countries.

In spite of limitations, Keynesian contribution to the development of economic theory can not be underestimated. There are few economists having their original ideas and conceptions like Keynes. The principle of effective demand continues to remain an important part of the modern macro-economic analysis.

QUESTIONS

1) State and explain Say's Law of Markets. How is it criticized by Keynes?
2) What is the effect of Wage-cut policy?
3) State briefly Say's Law of market.
4) Discuss the Classical theory of employment.
5) Explain the concept of wage price flexibility.
6) Discuss 'Supply creates its own demand'.
7) Explain fully the concept of effective demand.
8) Criticize the concept of effective demand.
9) What are the components of effective demand?
10) Give the outline of the Keynesian theory of employment.
11) Critically evaluate Keynesian theory of employment.
12) Explain the Keynesian model of underemployment equilibrium with the help of suitable diagram.

Chapter 8

PUBLIC FINANCE

CONTENTS

INTRODUCTION

"Public Finance" is that branch of general economics which deals with the financial activities of the state or government at national, state and local level. Economists, right from the classical times to the modern, have been influenced in determining the subject matter and scope of "Public finance" by their views regarding the role of the state in the life of nation.

The classical economists had advocated a Laissez-Faire philosophy in which the role of the state was limited. In fact, it was then believed that government is the best which governs the least. However, with the passage of time the governments have assumed greater responsibilities. The laissez-faire doctrine is now replaced by the concept of welfare of state. It was only during and after World War I that the theory of Public finance attained maturity and today it is recognized as a science by itself.

8.1 MEANING AND DEFINITIONS OF PUBLIC FINANCE

Public finance means the study of income and expenditure of Central, state and local government. Public finance is a fiscal science. In the traditional sense, public finance is a study of the nature and principles of state expenditure and state revenue. The word 'finance' signifies money matters and their management and 'Public Finance' in its modern sense presupposes the existence of a money economy.

Public finance is a branch of economics concerned with the identification and appraisal of the effects of government financial policies. It attempts to analyze the effects of government taxation and expenditure on the economic situation of individuals and institutions and to examine their impact on the economy as a whole.

According to R.A. Musgrave, "The complex of problems that centre on the revenue-expenditure process of government is referred to traditionally as public finance." The word Public Finance is a combination of two words, Public and Finance. Public is a collective name for the individuals living within an administrative territory. Public authorities include all sorts' government whether it may be central, state or local. The word Finance simply means income and expenditure.

According to Hugh Dalton, "Public Finance is one of the subjects, which lies on the borderline between economics and politics. It is concerned with the income and expenditure of public authorities and with the adjustment of one to other."

Fred Thompson defined Public Finance as, "Public Finance is the branch of public economics dealing with the revenue, budgeting and expenditure of governing agencies." He further explained the term public. The term Public has two meanings: 1) any group of more than one person; 2) the government sector of the economy. Usually, public finance deals with the second meaning, the finances of government as the agency representing the public.

According to Prof.Taylor, "Public finance is the fiscal science, its policies are fiscal policies, and its problems are fiscal problems."

The study of public finance is concerned with what are the sources of public revenue, items of public expenditure, constituents of the budget etc. The basic norm of modern public finance is general economic welfare. As an art, it enables the government to adopt the principles and policies in solving the financial problems of the government for the maximum benefit of the society. As a science, it teaches us the most economic and the best way to collect taxes and spend the revenue.

Nature of Public Finance

The nature of public finance can be explained as under:-

• Art as well as Science

Public finance is an art as well as science. It is a science as it denotes principles for public expenditure, public revenue, taxation and public debt. Application of these principles needs skill and social awareness. Hence it is an art as well as science.

- **Positive and normative science**

    Public finance has both its positive as well as normative aspect. In the positive aspect it studies and analyses the principles and problems of public revenue, public expenditure and public debt. In its normative aspect, the science of public finance evaluates the effects and consequences of fiscal operations of the state.

- **Fiscal Science**

    Public finance is finances by Government authorities in all levels from Local government to Central government. The finance of a government includes raising and disbursement of public funds. Thus, public finance is a study of nature and principles of Government expenditure and Government revenue. It is a fiscal science that denotes principles for raising and spending of public funds.

- **Budgetary policy**

    Each public authority has to prepare a budget and get it sanctioned from the relevant legislative authority. Normally, the budget is balanced is-so-far as the state or the local level authorities are concerned. However, whether the budget should be a balanced one, or a surplus one, or a deficit one depends upon the need of the economy and taking in to account the effects of each of these types of the budget, the decision regarding the national budget has to be taken.

- **Collective Wants**

    Human-being tries to satisfy all wants through individual efforts. But as human being live in society, it becomes necessary to satisfy some wants on the social level. Such wants are to be satisfied through social efforts are called as social wants or collective wants. Collective wants require public goods which are demanded by all members of the society equally and there cannot be any exclusion. The constructions of roads, railway, public health, maintenance of law and order, education, defence etc are some examples of social wants. These social wants are taken care of by the government which represents the society. These social wants are provided through the public budget.

Scope of Public Finance

The study of public finance can be broadly classified in to four categories:
- ➤ Public Revenue
- ➤ Public Expenditure
- ➤ Financial Administration
- ➤ Public Debt

(1) Public Revenue

Public revenue is raised essentially to meet the public expenditure. Fund raising by public authorities is an important part of the public finance. First of all, volume of public expenditure for the financial year is determined and then the required revenue is provided to meet that budgeted expenditure. The theory of public revenue includes the study of various sources of government income, their relative merits and demerits and principles governing the choice between them. Direct taxes, indirect taxes, fees, penalties, fines, profit of the public enterprise, grants are the important sources of public revenue.

(2) Public Expenditure

Public expenditure by public authorities is an important part of public finance. It creates base for future production and employment. It affects social life of the general public. It gives purchasing power to the economically weaker section of the society. It is also useful for creation of income equality. The theory of public expenditure includes a study of the principles, objectives and effects of public spending.

Public expenditure includes expenditure on administration of law and order, maintenance of police force and army, servicing public debt, provision of health care, development of basic industries, pollution control, infrastructural developments, providing public goods etc.

(3) Public Debt or Public Borrowing

In modern times public debt forms a major source of government funding both from the point of view of controlling the demand and of raising finances for implementing long term projects. Modern governments are taking resort to both internal and external debts.

When the Government becomes unable to meet its public expenditure through public revenue, it resorts to public debt. Public debt could be raised within the country or from foreign nations. Government may borrow from international financial institutions like World Bank, IMF etc.

(4) Financial Administration

Since in modern democracies the government operates at different levels, the financial problems and policies of the government at all levels are to be looked into. The preparation of budget, its implementation, the budgetary policy and its socio-economic effects are other important constituents of financial administration.

Public finance is a fiscal science and its scope is not limited only with the funds raising and funds disbursement activities of the Government, but government has to see that its expenditure and revenue are producing desirable effects and are controlling undesirable effects on the national income, production, employment and general well being.

Functions of public finance

The scope of public finance embraces the following major functions of the government's budgetary policy:

➤ **Allocation Branch**
➤ **Distribution Branch**
➤ **Stabilization Branch and**
➤ **Growth Branch**

Allocation Branch

Fiscal policy lies at the heart of the government's allocation function. Prof. Musgrave is of the opinion that public policy should intervene where market mechanism fails. Thus, the provision of social goods or public goods is always in government hands. In the same way, problems relating to social costs like pollution by factories can be regulated by the government by introducing appropriate economic legislation. Government intervention through appropriate economic legislation becomes necessary to minimize social hardships cost. The aim of the government is to have an optimum allocation of resources through budgetary operations.

Distribution Branch

The modern government intends to ensure a fair distribution of the country's income and wealth among the citizens. For this reason, a government tends to impose progressive taxes upon the richer sections so that there is equity in taxation and larger benefits to the poorer sections. Public finance aims at making use of taxation, expenditure and public debt policies to promote equitable distribution of income and wealth in the economy.

Stabilization Branch

It refers to the maintenance of a high level of resource utilization and stability of the value of money. In other words, full employment level and price stability are the important object of the government in modern public finance.

Growth Branch

It refers to the use of budget and fiscal instruments for the promotion of economic growth and development in the economy. The objective of growth with stability is important especially for a developing country like India.

8.2 PRINCIPLE OF MAXIMUM SOCIAL ADVANTAGE- DR. DALTON APPROACH

The principle has been introduced by well known British economist H. Dalton. Public revenue and public expenditure are two important financial operations of a state. These two financial operations of a state must be governed by some fundamental principles so that they may result in maximum social benefit. According to Dalton, the system of public finance is the best which secures maximum social advantage to the community. The state should always keep this principle while raising revenue or incurring expenditure.

The principle can be explained as under :

i) **Maximum utilisation of Resources :** An individual always attempts to maximize his satisfaction by using the resources available with him. On the same line, government also attempts to maximize social advantage by making proper utilization of its resources.

ii) **Social sacrifice :** When the Government recovers taxes or collects revenue from the public, there is social sacrifice. The tax payers make sacrifice of their purchasing power. The purchasing power goes to the Government.

iii) **Social Benefit:** When the Government spends on the activities, then the purchasing power is again transferred back to the society. Thus, public expenditure increases social benefits.

iv) **Social sacrifice shall be compared with social advantage :** Collection of revenue (taxes) from the public reduces their income and results in social sacrifice. At the same time, disbursement of the same revenue on public activities increases social advantage. It is not guaranteed that the only taxpayers will get the benefit from public expenditure. If the income of rich people is recovered by imposing income tax and then that income is used to provide necessities to poor people, it will result in maximising social advantage. Both the advantages and the disadvantages of public revenue and expenditure must be simultaneously considered.

v) **Equality of marginal sacrifice and advantage :** The principle of maximum social advantage implies that the public expenditure is subject to diminishing marginal social benefits and taxes are subject to increasing marginal social costs or sacrifice. There will be maximum social advantage when the marginal social benefits of public expenditure are equal to the marginal social sacrifice of taxation.

According to Dalton, "Public expenditure in every direction shared be carried just so far, that the advantage to the community of a further small increase in any direction is just counter balanced by the disadvantage of a corresponding small increase in taxation or in receipts from other sources of public expenditure or public income".

The government should plan its expenditure in such a way that the marginal unit of money spent on different item should give equal advantage. The last rupee spent on employment generation programme should yield a marginal social advantage equal to the last rupee spent on employment generation programme should yield a marginal social advantage equal to the last rupee spent on education or defence etc. In this way, when marginal advantage from spending on different heads becomes equal, then the social advantage becomes maximum. On the same line, when marginal sacrifice of all taxes becomes equal then minimization of social sacrifice will be achieved.

For maximization of social advantage, minimization of social sacrifice due to taxation and maximisation of social benefits from public expenditure is essential.

Graphical Representation

The principle of maximum social advantage can be graphically represented as follows :

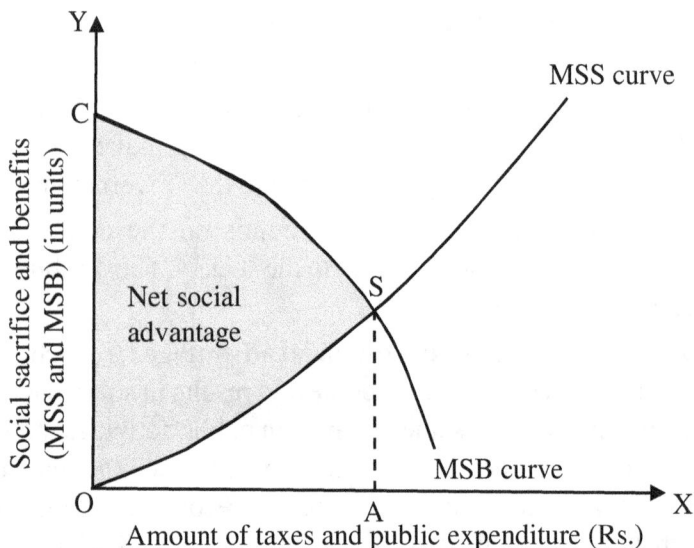

In the above diagram:

i)   'X' axis measures units of money recovered as taxes from public and in trun which is spent on public activities by the Governement.

ii) 'Y' axis measures social sacrifice and social benefits arisiing from collection of taxes and spending the revenue on public activities (i.e. MSS and MSB in unit).

iii) 'MSS' is the Marginal Social Sacrifice curve. It slopes upward to the right because with a rise in tax burden social sacrifice also rises.

iv) 'MSB' is a Marginal Social Benefit curve. It slopes downward to the right because a rise in public expenditure there arises fall in social benefits. Because rise in public expenditure decreases utility of every additional unit of money spent.

v)   'S' is a point where MSS and MSB curve intersect each other. At this point 'S', MSS from taxation equals to the MSB from the public expenditure (i.e. MSS=MSB). At this level of public finance, social advantage is maximum. In other words, 'OA' shows the level of taxation and spending by the Government, where social advantage is maximum, and it is equal to 'OC'.

Limitations of the Principle

Though the principle of maximum social advantage is considered as an ideal and the best guiding principle to the public finance activities, it has following limitations:

i) Measurement of social sacrifice and social benefit is practically difficult. These cannot be measurement of social sacrifice and social benefit is practically difficult. These cannot be measured accurately.

ii) The sacrifice and the benefit are relative concepts and they change with person to person. Therefore, maximum social advantage cannot be accurately measured.

iii) The concept of sacrifice and benefit, both change with change in time, place and situation. Therefore, accurate measurement of social advantage is impossible.

iv) It is very difficult to measure the marginal dissatisfaction of each individual separately from each additional tax.

Finally, we say that the principle of maximum social advantage shows an ideal level of taxation and spending by the government. It is the level, where MSS on account of taxation matches with the MSB accruing from public spending. At two level of taxation and spending by the government. It is the level, where MSS on account of taxation matches with MSB accruing from public spending. At two levels, the society gets maximum social advantage.

8.3 PUBLIC REVENUE AND EXPENDITURE

Pubic bodies raise funds to finance their activities from various sources; the most important being taxes and non-tax sources of revenue. We shall now throw some light on the various sources from which the government derives its income. Each of these sources is important as each has an impact on the production and distribution of wealth and each affects the level of economic activity and employment in the economy.

These sources can be very broadly divided in to two:
- Tax
- Non- tax

(1) Taxes

Every tax is a compulsory payment, without any direct and proportionate benefit to the tax-payer. Tax is a compulsory payment. Each on, without any distinction of caste, colour or age or sex has to pay it and the refusal to pay it entails punishment and even a delay in payment involve penalty. This makes a tax different from other sources. Tax imposes a personal obligation on the tax payer. Tax evasion and tax avoidance, both are punishable under law.

Tax paid by the person is utilized for meeting common needs and not for providing any direct service or benefit to the tax payer. At the same time the tax payer is not debarred from enjoying his or her share of the common benefit or general public services.

(2) Non-Tax Revenue

The first and the most important source under this head is the income earned from public enterprises and undertakings or the prices of goods and services produced and supplied by the government like postal stamps, electricity, gas, railway transport, telephone facility etc. Unlike taxes, prices are a voluntary payment, made by those who consume the goods and services and confer direct benefit to the payer of the price.

The second most important source under this category is the fee in various forms charged by the government for rendering service and for granting permission to perform a service. Some fees are charged for meeting the cost of administrative service rendered to confer special benefit to the fee payer.

The third most important source under his head is special levy to recover the cost of the project undertaken to improve civic amenities like construction of roads and parks, road lighting etc. A special levy is spent for special local project and it is levied on the basis of the benefit conferred.

Fines and forfeitures are another source of public revenue. Gifts and grants or donations from individuals or charitable organizations during natural calamities like earthquakes, famine, floods etc. also add to government revenue. In modern times, particularly after the Second World War, grants have become an important source of public revenue for developing countries. These have been known as 'Foreign Aid'. In a federal form of government, grants from the Centre to the States and from the States to the local governments are a common feature.

The theory and practice of taxation have undergone change with regard to its objective, nature, coverage and administration so as to make the tax system look better, effective and remunerative than before. Public revenue is raised essentially to meet the public expenditure.

Following are the main sources of public revenue:-

I. **Direct Taxes:** A direct tax is a tax, which is paid by the person on when it is legally imposed and the burden of which cannot be shifted to other persons. A direct tax includes income tax, wealth tax, property tax, gift tax etc. Direct taxes are one of the main sources of public revenue.

II. **Indirect Taxes:** Indirect taxes are those taxes which are levied on commodities either on their production or sales. At present indirect taxes have proved to be a significant source of revenue in developing country like India. It includes sales tax, excise duty, custom duty etc.

III. **Public Debt:** Public debt could be raised within the country or from foreign nations. Public debt plays a significant role in mobilizing resources for undertaking a higher volume of investment.

IV. Other sources of public revenue: other sources of public revenue include fees, penalties, fines etc. levied by the government. In addition to this, profits of the public enterprise, grants from one government to the other are the other important sources of public revenue.

Public Expenditure

Public expenditure is the expenditure incurred by public authorities- Central, State and local government for satisfying collective needs of the society and promoting the economic development and social welfare. During 19th century economists believed in laissez faire policy and argued that the government activities should be restricted to defense, law and order and public works activities only. However, since publication of Keynes General Theory of Employment, Interest and Money, public expenditure has become an important instrument for achieving and maintaining full employment in the economy. In developing countries public expenditure plays a key role in promoting economic development of the economy.

Classification of Public Expenditure

Public expenditure can be classified in to various categories, such as: -
  ➢ Revenue expenditure and capital expenditure,
  ➢ Developmental and non-developmental expenditure,
  ➢ Transfer payments and expenditure on goods and services

(1) Revenue expenditure and capital expenditure

Revenue expenditure is consumption expenditure incurred by the government and it is recurring in nature. It simply means that this expenditure does not lead to the creation of assets. On the other hand, capital expenditure is incurred on construction of building, roads, dams and buying machinery etc. which is not recurring in nature.

(2) Developmental and non-developmental expenditure

Developmental expenditure is that part of total government expenditure which is incurred for promoting economic development of the country. For example, expenditure on industries, agriculture, irrigation projects, construction of roads, railways, metro rail, bridges, are developmental expenditure. On the other hand, expenditure on administration, defense, interest on public debt etc are non-developmental expenditures.

(3) Transfer payments and expenditure on goods and services

Transfer payments are those kinds of expenditures against which there is no corresponding transfer of real resources. i.e. goods and services, to the government. For example, unemployment insurance, pensions, sickness benefits, interest on public debt etc. are non-developmental expenditure.

Expenditure incurred on buying goods and services is not transfer payment because in return of expenditure, government gets goods and services. Expenditure on defense, health, education etc. is non transfer expenditure as government obtains services of army personnel, doctor, teachers etc.

8.4 TYPES OF TAXATION

Taxes can be classified according to their nature, form, aim and methods of taxation. Generally taxes may be classified as below:
- ➢ Progressive, Proportional and Regressive taxes
- ➢ Direct and Indirect taxes

(A) Progressive, Proportional, Regressive taxes

Tax base is the object to which the tax applies such as the income or the value of a property. Tax rate is the amount of tax per unit of the tax base. The tax will be called proportional when the tax rate remains the same for each unit of the tax base. It will be progressive when the tax rate rises with every increase in the tax base. And it is regressive when the tax rate decreases with an increase in the tax base.

Progressive taxation is one in which the rate of tax goes on changing with changes in income. Under progressive method of taxation, both the rate of tax and the amount of tax paid by individuals vary in relation to their incomes. The progressive method of taxation is based on the principle of equality of sacrifice by all the tax payers. This method is introduced in order to maximize social welfare by redistributing wealth and income more equitably but it may discourage saving and investment.

In proportional method of taxation, every tax payer has to pay the tax at a flat rate, i.e. the rate of tax is the same for all the tax payers irrespective of their incomes. It is simple and uniformly applicable but rich and poor are taxed at the same rate.

In the Regressive method of taxation the rate of tax falls with the increase in tax base. Here as income goes on increasing the rate of tax goes on falling. From the point of view of the rate of tax, the burden of tax falls relatively heavily on poor and comparatively lightly on the rich. Taxes on necessaries are an example of regressive method of taxation. This method of taxation widens the area of inequality and is thus unjustifiable on the ground of equitable distribution of income and wealth.

(B) Direct and Indirect taxes

Taxes are compulsory contributions imposed by the Government on the citizens to meet its general expenses. Taxes may be classified as direct taxes and indirect taxes. According to Dalton, "A direct tax is really paid by the person on whom it is legally imposed, while an indirect tax is imposed on one person, but paid partly or wholly by another." This statement indicates that the distinction between direct and indirect tax is based on the concept of shifting. According to Dalton, if a tax is such whose burden cannot be shifted by the tax payer over to anyone else then such tax is a direct tax.

Whereas if a tax is such whose burden can be shifted, either partly or fully, by the initial tax payer over to anyone else then it will be regarded as an indirect tax.

A **direct tax** is a tax, which is paid by the person on when it is legally imposed and the burden of which cannot be shifted to other persons. A direct tax includes income tax, wealth tax, property tax, gift tax etc. Direct taxes are one of the main sources of public revenue. Income tax is charged under the Indian Income Tax Act, 1961. It is an annual tax on income of both individuals and companies levied by the union government. Every person, whose total income exceeds the maximum exemption limit, is chargeable to the income tax at the rates prescribed in the Finance Act passed each year by the parliament. Wealth tax is charged under the Indian Wealth Tax Act, 1957 and the Union government levies it. The tax is charged on individuals, Hindu Undivided Families and companies in respect of the net wealth held by them during the assessment year. Other taxes on capital and property are levied by the states and the local authorities.

Indirect taxes are those taxes which are levied on commodities either on their production or sales. The incidence or burden of these taxes can be shifted to other person and therefore these taxes are ultimately not paid by the person on whom they are levied. At present, indirect taxes have proved to be a significant source of revenue in developing country like India. It includes sales tax, excise duty, custom duty, service tax etc.

Advantages of Direct tax to Disadvantage of indirect taxes———-

Advantages of Direct Taxes

The main advantages of direct taxes are as follows.

I) Economy

The administrative cost of collection of these taxes is relatively lower, because the same officers who assess small income and property can assess larger incomes and properties also. The taxpayers make payment of taxes directly to the state treasury, hence all the amount of is deposited in the state treasury,

II) Certainty

In case of direct taxes, the taxpayer is certain about, how much amount he has to pay and at the sametime the state is also certain as to how much it has to receive income by way of the direct tax. As both the sides are certain, it tends to minimize corruption on the part of collecting officers.

III) Equity

Direct taxes are considered as just and equitable because they are based on progression so they fall heavily on rich persons than the poor people.

IV) Reduction in Inequalities

As the direct taxes are progressive in nature, they are charged at higher rates to the rich people, while poor people are exempted from direct tax obligations. Hence these taxes help in reducing inequalities in the distribution of income and wealth in the economy.

V) Elasticity

Direct taxes are elastic in nature, in the sense that, when the income of the people increases collection of direct taxes also increases. When tax rates are increased, government's total revenue also increases.

VI) Civic Consciousness

It is said that direct taxes help in increasing civic consciousness among the taxpayers. In a democratic country such civic consciousness also helps in checking the wastages in the public expenditure as he behaves as a responsible citizen.

VII) Productive

Direct taxes are very productive. As the society grows in terms of numbers and prosperity, the collection from direct taxes increases automatically. The direct taxes generally yield large revenue to the government.

Disadvantages of Direct Taxes

Direct taxes suffer from certain disadvantages as stated below.

I) Inconvenient

These taxes are inconvenient because taxpayer has to submit a statement of his total income as well as the sources of his income, which is generally complicated. These taxes are to be paid up in lump sum is also not convenient to the taxpayers.

II) Unpopular

The direct taxes are generally unpopular as they cannot be shifted and they pinch deeply to the taxpayers. They are opposed by the taxpayers.

III) Evadable

A direct tax is supposed to be a tax on honesty. An honest taxpayer does not evade it but many persons try to evade it through fraudulent practices. Generally there is lot of evasion incase of direct taxes.

IV) Possibility of Injustice

It is generally difficult to assess the income of all the classes accurately; hence direct taxes may not fall with proper weight on all classes. Even the tax rates of direct taxes are arbitrarily fixed by the government rather than fixing them on the basis of ability to pay.

V) Disincentive

If direct taxes are too heavy they tend to discourage saving and investment. As a result the economy may suffer heavily.

VI) Exemption of Low income Group

Under the scheme of direct taxes, low-income group people cannot be covered by the tax net. They are excluded on the basis of ability to pay and equity.

The direct taxes, however, are more advantageous and their limitations arise mainly on account of administrative procedure rather than on the grounds of fundamental principle. These limitations can be overcome through experience.

Advantages of Indirect Taxes

Indirect taxes have several advantages as follows.

I) Convenient

Indirect taxes are convenient to both, the taxpayers and the state. They are paid in small amounts and at intervals, when goods are purchased & these taxes are included in the price of the commodity, hence their burden is not felt by the taxpayers. They are also convenient to the government as they are generally collected from the manufacturers and importers.

II) Wide Coverage or Broad based

Indirect taxes cover both rich and poor people; hence they provide opportunity to every member in the society to contribute towards financing of the government for social services. They cover many products and many persons in the society so they are broad based, and they cover a larger section of the population.

III) Elastic

Indirect taxes are very elastic in yield, when imposed on necessities, which have inelastic demand; they tend to yield larger revenue. These taxes when levied on luxury goods cannot generate more revenue because demand for such goods is elastic.

IV) Non evadable

As Indirect taxes form a part of the price of the product, they cannot be evaded. However attempts may be made to evade these taxes through smuggling and maintaining false accounts

V) Can be made progressive

Indirect taxes can be made progressive by way of imposing heavy taxes on luxury goods and exempting commodities of mass consumption.

VI) Equitable

Indirect taxes can also be made equitable by imposing them, on luxury goods rather than on consumption goods.

VII) Productive

Indirect taxes are productive as income from them can be maximized by imposing few taxes, which yield a substantial amount of revenue, especially taxing essential commodities.

VIII) Checking harmful consumption

By way of imposing indirect taxes on harmful products, their consumption can be checked. For example, tobacco, wine and other intoxicants are taxed heavily.

IX) To reach the poor

Indirect taxation is the only means of reaching the poor people, to make them to contribute to the government finance. It is a sound principle that every individual should pay something to the government according to his ability to pay.

Disadvantages of Indirect Taxes

Some of the disadvantages of indirect taxes are discussed below :

I) Regressive

Indirect taxes generally fall more heavily upon the poor than upon the rich. So they are not equitable also.

II) Uncertainty

The income from indirect taxes is said to be uncertain because it is difficult for taxing authority to estimate accurately to total yield from different taxes, because the demand for different commodities, which are taxed, is influenced by many factors along with the price. Hence if the demand for goods taxed is elastic the income tends to be less and vice versa.

III) Uneconomical

The administrative cost of collection of indirect taxes is generally higher because large number of staff is required to administer these taxes. They are to be collected from a large number of people in very small amount, which becomes a costly process.

IV) Discouraging Savings

Indirect taxes tend to discourage savings because indirect taxes are included in price, which makes goods costly. As people have to spend more on essential commodities their savings tend to be lower.

V) Absence of Civic Consciousness

As these taxes are included in price, people do not know how much taxes they paying. These taxes are paid by middlemen like traders, they do not have direct impact. They are collected in small amount so they are not felt much by the taxpayers and hence civic consciousness is not aroused.

VI) Harmful to Industries

If raw materials are taxed, cost of production increases and the competitive capacity of industries decreases. Thus they are harmful to the industries.

VII) Inflationary

Indirect taxes tend to generate inflationary pressures in the economy.

It may be observed that neither the direct taxes nor indirect taxes can be said to be good or bad as each of them has its own merits demerits. No country can depend on one type of taxes. Modern government needs huge resources for carrying out its administrative, social and developmental activities. Hence it is desirable to have optimum combination of these two types of taxes. The rich may be covered by tax net through direct taxes and poor people through indirect taxes. Only care needs to be taken to see that taxes should be levied according to the ability to pay of the taxpayers, in order to avoid unfavourable effects of taxation policy of the government.

8.5 PRINCIPLES OF TAXATION

The principles underlying an ideal tax are called the canons of taxation.
Adam Smith has stated following **Principles or canons of taxation:**

1) Canon of Equality
This principle does not mean that every individual tax-payer must pay the same amount by way of tax, but every tax-payer must undergo equal sacrifice in the payment of tax. Every person will pay the taxes to the government in proportion to his ability to pay. Thus, to achieve greater equality, the tax must be progressive, i.e. the rate of tax must vary with the income of the tax-payer.

2) Canon of Certainty
According to Adam Smith, the tax which each individual is bound to pay ought to be certain and not arbitrary. The time of payment, the manner of payment, the quantity to be paid ought all to be clear and plain to the contributor, and to very other person. Besides this, the government must also be certain about the revenue that it is going to receive.

3) Canon of Convenience
Every tax should be levied in such a manner and at such a time that it provides maximum convenience to the tax payers.

4) Canon of Economy
The cost of collection of a tax should be as low as possible. Under no circumstances should the cost of collecting the tax exceed the amount of tax collected.

5) Canon of Productivity
The canon of productivity implies that a tax should yield sufficiently large revenue.

6) Canon of Simplicity
Taxes and tax system as a whole should be simple enough to be understood by every individual.

7) Canon of Diversity

With a view to ensuring that the tax burden is well spread over the entire citizen and that the element of inequality is the minimum the tax system must be diversified. This implies that different type of taxes must be introduced so as to cover each and every citizen.

8) Canon of flexibility

The tax system should have adequate flexibility so that a change in the tax structure, when needed, may be introduced without undue delay to meet the changing needs of the economy.

8.6 EFFECTS OF TAXATION

The term 'effect of taxation' refers to the changes in the economy generated by the tax system and its variations. In a market economy the taxation by influencing forces of demand and supply regulates the working of the market mechanism and in this process produces tremendous impact on all sectors of the economy.

We will now discuss the effects of taxation on the following areas:
- ➢ Effects of taxation on Production
- ➢ Effects of taxation on Distribution
- ➢ Other Effects of Taxation

(1) Effects of taxation on Production

The effects of taxation on production can be discussed as follows:

a) Effect on the ability to work, save and invest

Taxation result in the transfer of purchasing power from the private sectors to the government sector. Consequently the purchasing power in the hands of the individual tax payer is reduced and so his ability to purchase articles of necessaries, comforts and luxuries is also reduced. The effect is more prominent on the poorer sections of the society. Poor people have to reduce their consumption of necessaries and comforts and consequently their standard of living declines. This adversely affects their efficiency and ability to work. On the other hand, the tax does not affect so much the efficiency and ability to work of relatively rich classes because at the most the rich people are forced to reduce their expenditure on luxury goods which does not affect their efficiency and ability to work. Therefore, it is necessary that the burden of tax should be minimal on the poorer sections of the society so that their health, efficiency and ability to work are not adversely affected.

Looking at the effect of taxation from another angle we find that a tax on income will reduce disposable income of the people and since saving depend on income, these will automatically decline. In so far as the ability to invest is concerned, it entirely depends on savings. Since savings are reduced by taxation, ability to invest is obviously reduced. In short, taxation certainly affects the ability of the people to work, save and invest.

b) Effect of taxation on the Desire to work, save and invest

Taxation affects the incentive of the people to work, save and invest which in turn affects production. If the desire is strong then the people will work hard to save amore and invest more and consequently the production will automatically increase. However, people's desire to work, save and invest is determined by (i) The nature of taxes (ii) The psychological reaction the taxpayers.

(i) Nature of taxes

The ultimate purpose of taxation is to induce people to work hard and save more. Some taxes have bad effects and some have good effects on the tax payers desire to work and save. For example, taxes on windfall gains, inheritance tax, special assessment on the rise in land values etc. as these incomes are unexpected taxes on them do not affect the desire to work and save. Similarly, a moderate tax on commodities like excise duties and sales taxes will not adversely affect the producers' desire to work and save. But higher taxes on commodities tend to reduce demand for them due to higher prices; and hence output of such commodities will be reduced. Low export duties tend to encourage exports and hence production such goods may increase the desire to work, save and invest. Import duties help in protecting domestic industries and they may increase desire to work, save and invest more in production of goods which are imported.

(ii) Psychological reaction of tax payers

By psychological reaction we mean the immediate effect on the mind of the tax payers of the announcement of a new measure of taxation. It implies a change in the mental state of a tax payer by the imposition of a new tax or by the withdrawal of an old tax or by the imposition of a new tax or by the withdrawal of an old tax or by variations in the rate of the existing taxes. When a new tax is imposed or the rate of existing taxes is increased the tax payer's psychological feeling that the measure will adversely affect his income and therefore his desire to work hard and save more are adversely affected. This may be different on different persons. It depends upon the elasticity of demand for income for each tax payer.

(2) Effect of Taxation on Distribution

Dr. Dalton argues, "Other things being equal, one tax system is preferable to another, if it has a stronger tendency to check inequality." The effects of taxation on the distribution of income and wealth depend on two factors:
  ➢ Nature of taxation and tax rates
  ➢ Kinds of taxes

(A) Nature of taxation and tax rates

By nature of taxation means how the burden of taxation has been distributed among the different sections of the society. From the point of view of their nature, taxes have been classified in to three categories: Proportional, Progressive and Regressive. Under proportional taxation inequalities tend to remain the same if income remains constant. But if income changes in unequal proportion, then inequalities in income tend to increase.

The progressive taxes tend to decrease the inequalities in the wealth distribution as they fall more heavily on the rich.

Under regressive taxation, inequalities in the distribution of income and wealth tend to increase because the burden of taxes falls heavily on the poorer sections of the society. For example, a toll tax is regressive for the poor people.

Broadly speaking, taxes on income, property, articles of luxury are progressive in nature and taxes on articles of general consumption are regressive in their effect.

(B) Kinds of taxes

The effect of taxation is progressive, regressive or proportional in nature depends on the kind of taxes. All taxes can be broadly divided in to two classes: Direct taxes and Indirect taxes.

Direct taxes

Direct taxes are progressive in nature and fall heavily on the rich. Direct taxes based on the principle of progression and ability to pay falls heavily on the rich sections of the society. Hence they have socially favourable effects on distribution of income and wealth in a society. Take the case of income tax. A property tax can also be made progressive.

Indirect taxes

The burden of indirect taxes like taxes on mass consumption goods is regressive in nature because poor people have to spend larger part of their income on such goods as compared to that of rich people. The propensity to consume incase of poor people is relatively higher than that of the rich people. Such taxes lead to increase in inequalities of distribution of income in the society.

Since indirect taxes are imposed on commodities of mass consumption, their effect is regressive, because the taxes fall heavily on the poor. But all indirect taxes cannot be put in to this category. For example taxes on harmful products are beneficial from the point of view of the poor people but taxes on foodstuffs will be socially undesirable because they fall more heavily on the poor who spend larger proportion of their income on the consumption of foodstuffs.

(3) Other Effects of Taxation

Other effects of taxation are discussed as follows:

a. Taxation and Inflation

Taxation also has its effects on the level of prices. Indirect taxes have built-in-inflationary tendencies, whereas direct taxes are anti-inflationary in nature. Taxes may also be used effectively to regulate purchasing power and effective demand and thus provide a useful instrument to restore economic stability. During the period of prosperity, inflationary tendencies are dominant hence taxation helps in reducing purchasing power with the people. Imposition of new taxes and increasing existing rates of the taxes help in checking consumption and decreasing effective demand in the economy, so that price stability can be achieved.

b. Taxation and Employment

The taxation which reduce the general level of consumption and increases savings, will tend to reduce business activities and along with it employment in the economy especially in developed countries. Taxation which tends to discourage saving and investment will tend to reduce aggregate business activity and employment in developing countries. However, if this amount collected by way of taxes is spent by public authorities on public works or even on investment projects it would certainly create more employment.

c. Regulatory Effects of Taxation

The level of consumption and production in an economy can also be regulated with the help of taxation. The volume and nature of production can be regulated by imposing higher taxation on certain commodities and exempting production of certain other commodities. Similarly consumption and production of harmful commodities can be regulated by taxing them heavily. Likewise import and export duties may be used to regulate the volume of international trade and to protect the home industry from foreign competition. However mere taxation policy may not be effective and hence other supplementary measures such as fiscal policy may be used to regulate volume of production and consumption effectively.

8.7 CAUSES OF INCREASING PUBLIC EXPENDITURE

In modern times public expenditure has been increasing in all the countries of the world, because the activities of states are increasing steadily. Hence study of public expenditure has become important. There has been a spectacular increase in public expenditure in the course of last sixty years. Following are several reasons resulting in growth of public expenditure:-

1. Administrative Expenditure

A country which has accepted the democratic framework has to incur a very huge amount of expenditure on administration and maintenance of democratic institutions. The election and by-election procedures, the maintenance of several ministries at the Centre and at the State level etc have been certainly responsible for growing public expenditure on administration.

2. Defence Expenditure

The need for defence as well as for maintenance of law and order today is far greater than any time earlier. Manufacturing of modern defense weapons and maintenance of army has become costly affair. Technology progress has been much faster in defense equipment, which calls for adding new equipments to keep defense force up to date. All this has resulted in increase in public expenditure.

3. Inflation

On account of rising trend of prices, public expenditure in all the countries of the world is steadily increasing. With rise in price levels, government has to pay more for purchasing goods and services and has to pay for dearness allowance to its employees. This leads to increase in public expenditure all over the world.

4. Development of Agriculture

In case of a developing country like India, development of agriculture plays a key role in promoting economic development of the country. The Government has realized the close linkage between agricultural and non-agricultural sector. The interaction between these sectors contributes significantly towards economic progress of the nation.

5. Population Effect

In case of developing countries, population is increasing rapidly. Hence the government has to provide necessary facilities to increasing population. It has been observed that the public expenditure tends to increase in the same proportion at which population increases.

6. Urbanisation Effect

Higher rate of urbanization is also an important cause of increase in public expenditure. Expenditure on civil administration has increased beyond proportion in urban areas. As the government has to provide social services such as drinking water, sanitation facilities, maintenance of roads, traffic control, health, hygiene etc, these costs rise as population and size of urban areas increase. This results in increase in public expenditure.

7. Deficit Budget

Today almost all the countries of the world follow the norms of deficit budget instead of surplus or balanced budget. Deficit budget is one where the estimated government expenditure is more than expected revenue. Developing countries use deficit budget as a means to finance planned development. Developed countries use it as a stabilizing tool to control business and economic fluctuation. Deficit budget is useful to solve the problem of recession and depression which mainly due to lack of effective demand. But a very high deficit in the budget is not preferable as it creates inflationary pressure on the economy.

8. Non-plan Expenditure

Public expenditure may be classified in to Plan expenditure and Non-plan expenditure. A country like India is frequently the victim of natural calamities. Floods and famines regularly almost walk across the country. The government has to incur huge amount of expenditure by way of providing relief and recovery and implementing the rehabilitation programme.

9. Economic Development

The development efforts of the less developed countries have been responsible for the tremendous increase in public expenditure. It is not only that the overall plan outlay has been growing but there has been a very rapid increase in the growth of public sector outlay this accounts for a substantial increase in capital expenditure. Developing countries in the world are keen on attaining higher rate of growth to improve the standard of living of the people through the process of economic planning. To finance private sector the government has to establish development banks or financial institutions. As a result government expenditure increases rapidly.

10. Repayment of debt

One of the methods of financing huge expenditure is resorting to public debt. The repayment of debt along with huge amount of interest becomes a matter for concern because it is responsible for increase in public expenditure.

11. Infrastructure

The growing needs of expanding trade and commerce and industry require that the state must make adequate provision for quick and efficient mode of transport. A network of roads, railways, canals, electricity etc. must be set up. The creation of infrastructure involves huge public expenditure.

12. Welfare Economics

Governments are steadily increasing their activities especially welfare activities like education, public health, public recreation etc are supplied either free or at lower prices than their costs. Governments are incurring more and more expenditure on public works like railways, roads, bridges etc. to remove unemployment. Public expenditure in India, has contributed significantly towards socio economic development of the country.

_____

QUESTIONS

1) What is Public Finance?
2) What is maximum social advantage?
3) What are the principles of Taxation?
4) What is meant by progressive taxation?
5) What is direct tax? What are its advantages?
6) Write a note on Tax Revenue and Non-tax revenue.
7) How public expenditure is classified?
8) Discuss the effects of public expenditure on the economy.
9) What is Public Finance? Explain the nature and scope of Public Finance.
10) Explain the effects of taxation on production.
11) State and explain the principle of Maximum Social Advantage with its limitations.
12) What do you understand by public expenditure? Explain the causes of growth of public expenditure in modern times.

GLOSSARY

Aggregate demand - Sum of the values of all of the final goods purchased in an economy.

Aggregate demand (AD) curve - Relationship between the amount of goods and services people wish to purchase and the price level.

Aggregate demand schedule - Synonym for aggregate demand curve.

Aggregate supply (AS) curve - Relationship between the amount of final goods and services produced in an economy and the price level.

Aggregate supply - Aggregate demand model - Uniquely determines price level and level of output for which both goods and money market are in equilibrium.

Anticipated inflation - Inflation that people expect.

Anticipatory monetary policy - Monetary policy adopted in response to problems (i.e. inflationary pressure) that are expected to arise in the future.

Appreciation - Increase in the value of the domestic currency relative the currencies of other countries. Used when exchange rates are flexible.

Balance of payments - Measures the net flow of currency into the country from abroad.

Balance-of-payments deficit - Occurs when more money is leaving the country than is entering it.

Balance-of-payments surplus - Occurs when more money is entering the country than is leaving it.

Budget constraint - Limit to the amount of money an individual, a firm, or the government can spend. An individual's purchase might be constrained by his or her income (or wealth).

Budget deficit - The difference between the amount of money the government spends and the revenue that it receives in the form of taxes.

Budget surplus - Opposite of budget deficit.

Business cycle - Pattern of expansion and contraction of the economy.

Business saving - Saving by firms; profits not paid out to owners/stockholders.

Capital account - Net flow of dollars into the country resulting from the acquisition of domestic assets by foreigners.

Central bank - Bank that has control over the money supply. In the United States, the Federal Reserve. In Europe, the European Central Bank.

Composition of output - Relative amounts of consumption, investment, and government purchases that make up GDP.

Consumer durables - Consumer goods that yield services over a period of time; washing machines are an example.

Consumer price index (CPI) - Fixed-weight price index that measures the cost of the goods purchased by the typical urban family.

Credit rationing - Limiting the amount of money that individuals can borrow at the prevailing interest rate.

Credit targeting - Using monetary policy to achieve a particular level of debt.

Crowding out - Reduction in some component of aggregate demand-usually investment-that results from an increase ion government spending.

Current account - Net flow of dollars into the country resulting from the sale of domestic goods and services, and from net transfers from abroad.

Cyclical unemployment - Unemployment resulting from business cycle fluctuations.

Deflation - Rate at which the price level falls, in percentage terms; opposite of inflation.

Demand for real balances - Quantity of real money balances people wish to hold.

Depreciation - Decrease in the value of domestic currency relative the currencies of other countries; used when exchange rates are flexible.

Depreciation - Rate at which the capital stock wears out.

Devaluation - Decrease in the value of the domestic currency relative the currencies of other countries; used when exchange rates are fixed.

Discount rate - Interest rate charged by the Fed to banks that borrow money from it.

Disposable income - Income available for a household to spend; total income less taxes plus transfers.

Dissaving - Negative saving; borrowing/spending out of accumulated wealth.

Durable goods - Goods that yield services over a period of time. See consumer durables.

Equilibrium level of output - Level of output at which aggregate supply equals aggregate demand.

Equity - Share of ownership in a company; claim to a fraction of its profits.

Exchange rate - Price of foreign currency per unit of domestic currency.

Exogenous variable - Variable that is determined outside a particular model (whose value is independent of the values of a model's other variables).

Expansion - See recovery.

Face value - The amount that a bond pays its holder on expiration. The market value of a bond will equal its face value when the market interest rate is equal to the rate of return on the bond.

Factor payments - Payments made to factors of production; wages paid to labor are an example.

Factors of production - Inputs to production; capital, labor, and natural resources are examples.

Federal Reserve - The central bank of the United States. See Federal Reserve System.

Final goods - Goods that are sold to firms, the public, or the government for any purpose other than use as an input to production; all goods excluding intermediate ones.

Fiscal policy - Government policy with respect to government purchases, transfer payments, and the tax structure.

Fisher effect - Tendency of inflation and nominal interest rates to move together.

Flow variable - A variable that is measured in rates of change rather than levels. Contrast stock variable.

Frictional unemployment - Unemployment associated with the movement of workers in and out of jobs in "normal" times.

GDP deflator - Measure of the price level obtained by dividing nominal GDP by real GDP.

GDP gap - Difference between potential GDP and actual GDP. See output gap.

GDP per capita - GDP per person.

Globalization - Notion that the world is moving toward a single global economy.

Government budget deficit - Excess of government expenditure over government revenue.

Government expenditure - Total government spending; includes both government purchases and transfers.

Government saving - Saving by the government; the difference between the revenues taken in (i.e., from taxes) and the money used/given away (i.e., transfer payments, interest payments on the national debt).

Great Depression - A historical period of very low output and very high unemployment that occurred during the years 1929-1941 in the United States. A number of other countries also experienced severe depressions during this period.

Gross domestic product (GDP) - Measure of all goods and services produced within the country in 1 year. Real GDP measured in units of constant value. Nominal GDP measured in dollars.

Gross national product (GNP) - Measure of the value of all final goods and services produced by domestically owned factors of production.

Growth rate - Rate at which a variable increases in value; percentage change in the level of a variable.

Growth theory - Tries to explain why output grows over time, and to identify the factors that affect it growth rate.

High-powered money - Currency (notes and coins) and banks' deposits at the Fed; also called the monetary base.

Human capital - Education and training of individuals to increase productivity.

Hyperinflation - Very rapid price increase, usually defined as over 100 percent per month.

Indicators - Economic variables that signal us as to whether we are getting close to our desired targets.

Inflation - Percentage rate of increase in the general price level.

Inflation targeting - Using monetary and fiscal policy to achieve a particular rate of real GDP growth.

Instruments - The "tools" policymakers manipulate directly to affect the economy.

Intermediate goods - Goods used to produce other goods or services; flour purchased by bakers is an example.

Investment - Purchase of new capital, principally by the business sector.

Keynesian aggregate supply curve - Horizontal aggregate supply curve.

Liquid assets - Assets that can be easily and quickly converted into the unit of account (dollars in the United States). Easily used to make transactions.

Liquidity - A measure of the ability to make funds available on short notice.

Liquidity constraint - Limitations on ability to borrow in order to finance consumption plans.

Liquidity trap - Horizontal curve due to extreme interest sensitivity of money demand.

Long run - Period of time long enough for prices to clear all markets so that output is equal to potential output, but short enough for potential output to be fixed. In general a period of decades or more, over which potential output is expected to grow.

Medium of exchange - One of the roles of money; asset used to make payments.

Misery index - Index used by political analysts to measure people's unhappiness with the dual problems of inflation and unemployment; the sum of inflation and unemployment.

Money (money stock) - Assets that can be used for making immediate payment.

Money illusion - Belief that the numbers used to express prices have significance- that changes in the nominal price of a good are meaningful in and of themselves.

Multiplier - Increase in endogenous variable for each $1 increase in exogenous variable; particularly, increase in GDP for each $1 increase in government purchases.

National income - Total payments to factors of production; net national product minus indirect taxes.

Natural rate of unemployment - Rate of unemployment at which the flows into and out of the unemployment pool balance; also the point on the augmented Phillips curve at which expected inflation equals actual inflation.

Net domestic product (NDP) - GDP minus allowance for depreciation of capital.

Net exports - Exports minus imports.

Neutrality of money - Proposition that equiproportional changes in the money stock and prices leave the economy unaffected.

New classical economics - Belief that the private economy is inherently efficient and that the government ought not to attempt to stabilize output and unemployment.

New Keynesian economics - Models whose basis is rational behavior and conclude that the economy is not inherently efficient and that, at times, the government ought to stabilize output and unemployment.

Nominal GDP - Value of all final goods and services produced in the economy; not adjusted for inflation.

Nominal money supply - Nominal value of bills and coins in circulation; says nothing about the amount that these bills and coins can purchase.

Open economy - An economy that trades goods, services, and assets with other countries.

Open market operation - Federal Reserve purchase or sale of Treasury bills in exchange for money.

Optimal - Best

Personal saving - Saving by individuals and families.

Phillips curve - Relation between inflation and unemployment; in a sense, a dynamic version of the aggregate supply curve.

Policy mix - Combination of fiscal and monetary policy to achieve both internal and external balance.

Political business cycle theory - Theory that politicians deliberately manipulate the economy to produce an economic boom at election time.

Portfolio - The mix of assets someone owns.

Portfolio disequilibrium - Occurs when people are holding more of some asset (i.e., money) at the prevailing interest rate than they wish to.

Potential output - Output that is produced when all factors are fully employed.

Precautionary motive - A reason people hold money; they do not know how much they'll need to spend.

Private saving - Saving by individuals, by families, and by firms; saving by everyone other than the government.

Producer price index (PPI) - Price index based on a market basket of goods used in production. The PPI replaced the wholesale price index (WPI).

Production function - Technological relation showing how much output can be produced for a given combination of inputs.

Quantity theory of money - Theory of money demand emphasizing the relation of nominal income to nominal money. Sometimes used to mean a vertical LM curve.

Real balance - Real value of the money stock (number of dollars divided by the price level).

Real business cycle (RBC) theory - Theory that recessions and booms are due primarily to stocks in real activity, such as supply shocks, rather than to changes in monetary factors.

Real exchange rate - Purchasing power of foreign currency relative to the U.S. dollar.

Real GDP - A measure of output; adjusts value of final goods and services to reflect changes in the price level.

Real interest rate - Return on an investment measured in dollars of constant value; roughly equal to the difference between the nominal interest rate and the rate of inflation.

Real money supply - Real value of the bills and coins in circulation; equal to the nominal money supply divided by the price level.

Recovery - A sustained period of rising real income.

Required-reserve ratio - Fraction of a bank's deposits that it is required to keep on reserve.

Reserve ratio - Ratio of bank reserves to bank deposits; a primary determinant of the money multiplier.

Reserve - Part of a bank's deposit kept at the Fed, or in its vaults; money that a bank keeps on hand instead of lending out.

Saving - Money that is not spent.

Short run - A period of time short enough that markets are unable to clear, so that output can deviate from potential output.

Speculative motive - A reason people hold money; although the return on holding money is small, people hold it because it reduces the risk associated with their portfolio of assets.

Stagflation - Simultaneous inflation and recession.

Standard of deferred payment - Asset normally used for making payments due at a later date.

Store of value - Asset that maintains its value over time.

Structural deficit - Deficit that would exist with current fiscal policy if the economy were at full employment. Formerly called "high-employment' or "full-employment" deficit. Contrast cyclical deficit.

Supply shock - An economic disturbance whose first impact is a shift in the aggregate supply curve.

Supply-side policy - Policy that causes the aggregate supply curve to shift.

Targets - Indentified goals of policy.

Tariff - A tax imposed on imported goods.

Transactions motive - A reason people hold money-we use it to purchase goods and services.

Transfer payments - Money given by the government to individuals, not in exchange for goods or services; welfare payments are an example. See also entitlement programs.

Unemployed person - A person who does not have a job but is actively seeking one.

Unit of account - Asset in which prices are denoted.

Velocity of money - The number of times the rupee changes hands during the year.

Very long run - A period of decades or more, over which potential output is expected to grow.

REFERENCES

1. Ahuja H. L., 2008 - Macroeconomics – Theory and Policy, Edn-14th, S.Chand & Company

2. Dalton Hugh, 1978 - Principles of Public Finance, Edn- 4th, Allied Publishers Pvt. Ltd.

3. Dornbusch R., Fischer S. & Startz R., 2002 - Macroeconomics, Edn-8^{th,} Tata McGraw-Hill

4. Extra Issue on General Studies INDIAN ECONOMY, 2011-12, Revised Edition, Pratiyogita Darpan

5. Gordon E. and Natarajan, 1999 - Banking – Theory, Law and Practice, Edn-14th Revised, Himalaya Publishing House

6. Gupta Suraj B., 2006 - Monetary Economics, 2006 Reprint, S. Chand & Company

7. Hajela T.N., 2010 - Public Finance, Edn- 4th , Ane Books Pvt. Ltd.

8. Jain T. R. and Ohri V. K., 2010-11- Introductory Microeconomics and Macroeconomics, Edn-2010-11, V. K. Global Publications Pvt. Ltd. New Delhi

9. Jhingan M. L., 2010 - Macro Economic Theory, Edn-12th, Vrinda Publications

10. Kulkarni Kishore G., 1999 - Modern Monetary Theory, Edn-1st, Macmillan India Limited

11. Lipsey Richard & Chrystal K. Alec, 1999 - Principles of Economics, Edn- 9th, Oxford University Press

12. Mansfield Edwin, 1998 - Essential Macroeconomics Principles, Cases, Problems, Edn- 1st, W.W. Norton & Company, Inc.

13. Paithankar Dr. R. G. and Datar Pradeep V., 2005 - Business Economics-II (Macro), Edn-1st, Diamond Publications

14. Rangarajan C. & Dholkia B. H., 2006 - Principles of Macroeconomics, 31st Reprint, Tata McGraw-Hill

15. Samuelson P.A. and Nordhaus W.D., 2002 - Economics, Edn-17^{th,} Tata McGraw-Hill

16. Singh Supreet and Gupta Anil K., 2012 - Public Finance, Dominant Publisher & Distributors Pvt. Ltd.

17. Special Issue on INDIAN ECONOMY, 2010-11, Dhankar Publications Pvt. Ltd., Meerut (UP)

18. Worswick David & Trevithick James, 1983 - Keynes and the Modern World, Cambridge University Press

www.ingramcontent.com/pod-product-compliance
Lightning Source LLC
Chambersburg PA
CBHW081324020726
47506CB00005B/1170